The Hunge

J. M. Hewitt

© J M Hewitt 2016

J M Hewitt has asserted her rights under the Copyright, Design and Patents Act, 1988, to be identified as the author of this work.

First published by Endeavour Press Ltd in 2016.

This books is dedicated to the memory of my grandmothers; Daisy Wozny and Ivy Hewitt. Both avid readers who would have enjoyed my tale.

Table of Contents

Chapter 1	9
Chapter 2	11
Chapter 3	15
Chapter 4	17
Chapter 5	27
Chapter 6	34
Chapter 7	39
Chapter 8	48
Chapter 9	52
Chapter 10	60
Chapter 11	64
Chapter 12	70
Chapter 13	85
Chapter 14	96
Chapter 15	101
Chapter 16	109
Chapter 17	111
Chapter 18	114

Chapter 19	117
Chapter 20	119
Chapter 21	122
Chapter 22	126
Chapter 23	128
Chapter 24	130
Chapter 25	133
Chapter 26	137
Chapter 27	139
Chapter 28	143
Chapter 29	145
Chapter 30	147
Chapter 31	149
Chapter 32	152
Chapter 33	154
Chapter 34	158
Chapter 35	160
Chapter 36	162
Chapter 37	165
Chapter 38	167
Chapter 39	170

Chapter 40	172
Chapter 41	174
ACKNOWLEDGEMENTS	176

Chapter 1

February 1981

The garden. When they had moved in ten years ago she had such dreams about the garden. She was going to grow sweet pea and amaryllis in the spring, and freesia and hydrangeas in the summer. At the back, down near the railway track, she planned to grow seasonal vegetables and set up a swing or a slide for the children they would inevitably have.

How young she had been back then. How stupid.

As one year rolled into the next she had berated herself every time she stood at the kitchen sink and looked out at the garden. It was unavoidable to look outside; after all, she positioned herself in that spot at least twice a day to do the washing up. Eventually she had solved the issue of staring at the barren, concrete wasteland by purchasing some green material from town, borrowing her mother's sewing machine and making a curtain. The green cotton was ideal. By squinting or half closing her eyes she could almost be looking at the lush garden paradise she had envisioned. She had never given the machine back, which had led her doing alterations here and there for people who were willing to pay. The pin money came in handy and whatever she made she kept concealed in the rear of the sewing machine, in the part where the back came off and you were supposed to store bobbins and reels of cotton.

The curtain serves another purpose. When it is drawn across, not only does it prevent her from looking at the crudely cemented exterior, but also from her seeing her own reflection in the window. Bronwyn used to love looking at herself in the mirror, when she was a young girl, before her face got lined and her shoulders sagged with the weariness of life. Her hair is still long but it used to be sleek and as black as a raven's wing. Now it's dull, like her skin and her life. Preening, was what her mother used to say she was doing. Danny used to look at her looking at herself in the looking glass with an expression of satisfaction and pride. These days, the only looks he shoots her are glances of annoyance and distaste.

It's the kid thing, she thinks, the reason why they fell apart. Though they never prevented it no baby ever came. Dan refused to go for tests, an insult on his manhood or some such rubbish, so they just carried on. Barren, just like the garden.

She can hear him stirring now and automatically she glances at the clock. It's already dark out, almost 6 p.m and he's only now getting up. He was out late last night and he has slept all day. She doesn't know who he was with or what he was doing. He doesn't offer up any information. She doesn't ask.

He thumps down the stairs and scuffs into the kitchen. She appraises him; she still looks at him. He is still a good looking man. The years have been kind to him and it needles her. They live the same life, eat the same food, smoke the same amount of cigarettes. He doesn't exercise, but his arms are toned and his shoulders are muscled. She feels her lip curl.

"Make us a tea?" he asks.

She slings the tea towel into the sink. "Do you know what time it is?"

He grunts, hawks something up in his throat and spits it into the sink.

"Jesus," she whispers, feeling her lip curling again.

"What?" he rasps, opening the fridge and leaning into it. "Fuck sake, any chance of you going shopping sometime soon, Bron?"

He emerges and she turns to the kettle, flicks it on and takes a deep breath. "With what? You need money to buy food. Have you got any?"

He whips a T-shirt from the clothes horse standing in front of the three bar electric fire and pulls it over his head. Without another word, he snatches up his keys and slams his way out of the house.

Chapter 2

Across town Rose James hurries along the street. Head down, dark blonde hair shielding her face. She pauses and, pushing her fringe out of her eyes, she looks up at the sky. It's a clear night, but bitterly cold. Winter will soon be drawing to a close and she longs for the spring warmth. Though with the new season comes more sunlight. The only good thing about these long nights is the darkness that she uses like a cloak. Less hours of twilight mean less time to spend with Connor, but she won't think of that, not now, not on her way to see him. It's hard though, hiding like this. And they shouldn't have to sneak around, it shouldn't matter, so what if she's a Catholic and he's a Protestant. They like each other, and neither of them goes to church anyway. But she knows everyone else won't see it through rose tinted glasses the way she does. And now, as Rose hurries through the dark streets, glancing around lest anybody should see her, she wonders whether she is doing the right thing.

"But you always wonder that," she mutters to herself as she crosses the park. "And you keep on bloody doing it anyway."

She hates walking through here alone to meet him, but she will never tell Connor that. The dread starts as soon as she leaves her home, a tight ball in the pit of her stomach, convinced that with every step she takes one more person is looking out of their window or poking their head out of their front door, until eventually it seems that the whole of her neighbourhood has fallen into step behind her, knowing what she is doing, where she is going, who she is seeing. But then she'll see him – Connor standing in the shadows, his handsome features half hidden in the moonlight, seemingly lost in his own thoughts, until she makes her presence known and then he grins, and she knows never, ever could she leave him, no matter what the risks.

It happens now, as she reaches the most easterly point of Church Street and sees him sitting on the wall of one of the back gardens. He holds up a hand in greeting and she steps up her pace and waves back, her heart beating ever faster and a ridiculous grin on her face.

She pulls up sharply six feet away from him and his smile fades. What is it? She asks herself, silently, as there *is* something. Footsteps? Voices in a hushed whisper? She doesn't know, but something is off. She is about to call to him to come to her and then they appear behind him, suddenly and silently, as though they had been there the whole time. Black clothed apparitions, their intentions already clear to her from the ski-masks that they wear.

She sees her hand come out, as though to reach over to him and pull him across to her. Instead, the world tilts and she swings her arm to her left until the cold brick of a garden wall scrapes her fingertips.

"No!" She thought she yelled it but she hears the replay in her mind and it was a whisper, snatched away by the wind.

She hardly notices one of the three men running towards her, but there he is, at her side, his right arm gripping her slim waist, his left hand roughly holding her face at such an angle that she has no choice but to see.

A dreadful howl rings through the silent night as a shot blasts from somewhere, from someone. Rose honestly doesn't know if it were her or Connor who screamed so terribly.

The shooter speaks to Connor, his voice low and guttural, too quiet for Rose to hear his words.

He stands, turns towards Rose.

"Keep a hold of her," he says, louder this time, and as he moves towards her he kicks at Connor's inert body.

Thoughts of her best friend, Bronwyn swirl around her head and fear lends her a strength that she didn't know she had as she twists out of the man's grasp, aims her foot high like Bronwyn had taught her, and catches the lad where it hurts him most with her boot.

As she runs her feet barely skim the pavement as she rips through the gardens and back alleys she has come to know so well. Over low level walls she leaps, not daring to stop, almost feeling the breath of her pursuers on the back of her neck, tearing through the washing that hangs on the lines, not caring when she got caught up in frost laden stiff sheets and they trail across the gardens behind her. She is literally running for her life.

Finally she stops and slumps to the ground behind a dustbin. Tears sting her eyes and she heaves as the horror of what happened replays in her mind.

Connor has been *shot*! Had he been shot? She heard a gun fire, she thinks she recalls wisps of smoke, curling from a barrel, but at that moment she doesn't know what is fact and what is fiction in her ever hopeful head.

But Connor doesn't own a gun, the masked men always do and she knows the way it works, he would have been left there, in the road, all of the time losing more blood.

She pushes herself up and staggers back to the fence that she had just hurled herself over. No longer having any regard for her own safety, she starts to make her way back to the border.

*

A curtain is moved aside and a pool of light falls onto the street where the three lads are working Connor over.

Curtain twitching is not an uncommon occurrence, and the person who dared to look normally did not approach, even if it were one of their own. But this time the curtain belongs to Connor's mother, Mary, and as she realises that it is her boy on the cobblestones she lets out a strangled cry. Memories of another incident in another time pulse through her head as she struggles with the catch, recollections tripping over themselves in her head, crushing her thudding heart in her chest. At the same time as the window flies open the emotions tear up her throat and, with no words forming in her mind, she leans out of the window and screams hard and long into the night.

The three men simultaneously look up and pause. Mary continues to scream, and her inability to find her power of speech eventually frightens her into silence. For a long moment they look at each other, then, as Connor rolls over and raises his head, they all look down at him as he speaks hoarsely.

"Ma, don't you come out here."

Mary Dean either doesn't hear or heed her son's warning; all that matters is stopping the three men before they kill him. The man who holds the shotgun appraises the situation rapidly. He seems to decide that the woman in the window is no threat and turns back to the task at hand. Mary, shocked to her core by the past memory that mingles into the present day, grabs onto the terrible night that happened over twenty years ago that she never lets herself think about. She drags it into the forefront of her mind, makes herself visualise it, though she doesn't need to because it's happening again, right now in front of her. But this time it's happening to her son and it's all she needs to make her body obey the commands that her brain is issuing. She pulls herself up onto the window ledge and swings her legs over. As if encouraged by Mary's bravery, several more windows open in the neighbouring houses. The three men look at each other and with a silent communication born from years of practice they know it is time to leave. Their work done anyway, they melt away into the night as Mary hurries over to Connor.

*

When Danny climbs into bed, Bronwyn stirs.

"It's only me," he whispers. His voice is soft and contrite, so unlike the normal, barking tone he uses with her these days that she reaches over to switch on the lamp.

She blinks as her eyes became accustomed to the light.

"What's that on your face?" she asks, before looking away.

He swipes at his cheeks and peers at his fingers. "Shit," he swears softly, and gets back out of bed.

Bronwyn lies down and listens to him in the bathroom.

A thousand questions run through her head. Where has he been? Who has he been with? The same questions she has most nights, repeated on a loop. But she'll never ask him because he'll never tell her.

Bronwyn slides out of bed and pads silently to the bathroom where she peers through the crack between the hinges of the half open door. In the harsh lighting she sees Danny as he scrubs at his face with a towel. He strips his clothes off and crumples them up, throwing them to one side. Though he stands naked, she lets her gaze drift over to the balled up clothes. A murmur from him snaps her attention back and she inhales sharply as Danny smiles at himself in the mirror. His hands move down his body, stop, and in the reflection she sees him take himself in his hands. Covering her mouth, she hurries back to the bedroom.

Chapter 3

February 1981

This house is cold. It's so cold that even doubling up the duvet and wrapping myself in it like the Michelin man doesn't warm me up.

"Bron," I call, and wait, but she doesn't reply.

I root around for last night's socks but pulling them on makes no difference so I grab Bronwyn's pillows and heap them on top of me. I'm so sick of living like this, in a cold house with an empty fucking fridge. Maybe it's time for Bronwyn to go back to work.

She wasn't ever going to work. When we got wed it would only be a matter of time before the kids came along, so there didn't seem much point in her starting up anywhere. I was earning an okay wage as a pipe fitter. Money was tight, but back then we didn't need much. We had each other. Fuck, what happened to that? What happened to those days when I would come home at the end of a shift and she would ask me what I wanted for dinner? I would tell her, fuck dinner, and I'd fuck her instead.

We had a real fire back then and on Sunday afternoons in the winter we would walk through the Guillion forest and collect bits of wood. We didn't think we were allowed to do this so we'd stuff as many pieces as we could into out bags and get the bus, running home from the bus stop, giggling like little kids. We bought an electric fire one winter and stood it in the hearth. We stopped collecting wood after that.

I'm no warmer and I curse this fucking house. It's an end of terrace, if we'd got a middle one we'd have heat from the dwellings either side, and to make it worse our bedroom is on the side that has no house next to it. Maybe we should move our bed into the second bedroom. We were saving it for a nursery but there's not much chance of needing it now. Not that I mind, kids get on my nerves anyway and Bronwyn hasn't got much interest in the whole family thing anymore. She doesn't need babies hanging off her; she's got me, and I'm enough for any lass.

The second bedroom is smaller, but at least it would be warmer.

Jesus, I don't want to get up yet, but I can't sleep in this chill. I poke my leg out and bang on the floor with my heel.

I'll get Bronwyn to bring the kitchen fire up and plug it in. That'll warm me up.

But no matter how much I thump the floor with my foot and shout for her to bring me the fire and a cup of tea, she doesn't come.

Chapter 4

February 1981

Rose is still two streets away when the flashing blue lights fall upon her, creating long blue shadows that fade in and out over the road. She quickens her step until she arrives back at the spot where Connor had been shot and stares aghast at the crowd of people surrounding the ambulance. For a moment she hesitates before forcing her feet to move. She skirts around the crowd, back and forth, unable to find an opening. Panicking, with tears streaming unchecked down her face, she elbows her way through and, as Connor is being lifted into the ambulance, she runs up to the door.

He has an oxygen mask on and she clutches at the door of the ambulance, needing to feel something solid in a world that is tipping on its axis. A virtual river of blood from his leg has left a trail on the ground and, for a heart-stopping second, she thinks that he is dead. But he wouldn't have an oxygen mask on if he's dead, she tells herself.

He opens his eyes, they focus on her. She smiles through her tears, but it smiles when he doesn't respond. Finally, he lifts a hand in her direction. Is he waving her away, or beckoning to her? She can't tell but she puts a foot on the step and a strangled, thick sounding cry escapes from her as she is suddenly pulled back. For a moment she believes the crowd has her in their clutches, they have turned on her, are holding her responsible for the shooting of their neighbour. She wrenches herself free and spins around, gulping for air against the sobs.

"What are you doing? Who are you?" A tall lady with fire in her eyes that match her red hair shouts down into Rose's face.

"Ma, please…," Connor pulls the oxygen mask off his face. "Leave her alone."

Mary glances at her son and looks back at Rose.

For a moment the two stare at each other, the crowd are silent though their hostility is palpable. Rose slowly edges back towards the ambulance. Gritting her teeth she hauls herself up and in and moves up to Connor's head. Mary looks at them both for a moment and Rose holds her breath. She knows about Mary Dean, Connor has told her all about Mary. How strong she is, protective and loving. When he talks about his mother the light shines from his face and Rose always feels a pinch of envy. Her own mother could never be described like that.

Mary seems to decide not to pull Rose out of the ambulance and finally she climbs up inside as well.

The ride to the hospital is fraught with tension. Rose sits beside Mary, silent tears rolling down her cheeks. Connor slips in and out of consciousness while the paramedics work, fixing drips to him and checking his vital signs.

At the hospital, Mary and Rose are left alone. With Connor not there, they have to acknowledge each other.

"How long have you been with him?" Mary asks in her thick Irish brogue.

"Six months." Rose stares down at the carpet.

Mary says nothing but watches Rose quietly for a while. Rose can quite imagine that she's wondering what is so special about her that Connor would risk his life for. And the answer is; nothing. There is nothing special about Rose, she can hardly believe Connor was ever interested in her. She is quiet, plain, dull, even.

"Connor's dad was a Catholic," says Mary, and Rose looks up in surprise.

"I didn't know that, isn't he—?"

"Dead. Yes, that he is." Mary looks Rose straight in the eye. "Killed by his own men, *your* men, 'cause he was with me."

Rose looked back down to the floor at Mary's words, spoken so matter of factly.

"They wanted me out, they wanted to run me out of town but I stuck it out, raised my boy, worked hard. Nobody bothers me now."

"I'm sorry," says Rose, and she's not sure if she's expressing her condolences for Connor's father's death, or apologising for bringing trouble to Mary's door again. And she wonders why they don't bother her now? Does Mary lead such a solitary life that generation's past have forgotten that she even exists?

"But can you stick it, girl?" Mary's eyes glint in the dim light of the room. "Sitting there, looking like a deer caught in the headlights, looking like you wouldn't say *boo* to a goose. If your family threw you out and your friends spat at you in the street, could you handle it?"

Rose raises her head and meets Mary's gaze head on.

"I could. I can. I love your son, Mrs Dean, and I'll give up anything for him. We'll move away from here to somewhere where stupid politics don't matter. I *can* handle it."

Mary laughs; a harsh, brittle sound without any humour.

She doesn't answer. She doesn't believe Rose.

*

It's dawn when Rose leaves the hospital. When news had come from the operating theatre that Connor was going to be okay, she made her promises to Mary that she would return that evening.

Mary had not commented, hadn't even looked at her and with a whispered goodbye Rose had fled.

Standing in the bus shelter Rose slumps at the thought of going home. Her mother, who she lives with, is worse than Mary Dean with her rage. News will have spread and she can't face her mother. Not yet. There's only one safe haven left to her. The same haven she has used since childhood.

Bronwyn's.

*

Though the sun has not yet fully risen Bronwyn is up and on her second coffee. She stands in her usual spot, looking at the green curtain, sipping from her mug and thinking about Dan in the bathroom last night at the same time as trying not to think about it.

An urgent hammering on the front door shatters the morning silence and she jumps, slopping coffee over her hand.

"Jesus," she hisses, clutching at her scalded hand and hurries to open the door before the racket wakes Dan.

Before the door is even fully open a small, brown shape squeezes in and lurches through to the kitchen.

"Rose!" Bronwyn closes the front door and goes into the kitchen. Rose has sunk into the kitchen chair and put her head in her hands. "What in hell has happened to you?"

"I went to meet Connor, just as I got there some lads jumped him." She looks up at Bronwyn, her eyes red and puffy. "They grabbed me, they made me watch…" Rose clamps her hand over her mouth and scraping her chair back, she staggers across the kitchen and vomits into the sink.

Bronwyn closes the kitchen door softly and goes to her friend, rubbing her back.

"Did they hurt you?"

"No, I got away," Rose turns on the tap and the women watch as the water swirls around the sink. "They shot Connor. They kneecapped him."

The hysterics are over. Both Bronwyn and Rose have lived all their lives with shootings on their doorstep. It's like a cancer, everyone knows someone who has been shot, bombed, beaten. Rose should know better than to get in with a Prod, it's risky, life threatening – for both parties - and she knows that.

"Is he worth it? Really, I mean," Bronwyn asks as she leads Rose back to the table.

"Yeah, he is." Rose reaches across the table and grabs Bronwyn's hand. "I've never had this before, not with anyone."

Maybe that's the problem. Rose is so inexperienced that she's gladly accepted the first man who has looked at her. Bronwyn hasn't met Connor, all she has is Rose's words of praise about the man.

"What, would you not fight for Dan, if you couldn't be together, if society was keeping you apart?" Rose, still clutching Bronwyn's hands, is imploring her to understand. But she's chosen the wrong example and Bronwyn pushes Rose away and puts her own hands under the table.

"I don't think I'd fight for anything anymore."

Bronwyn gets up and goes to the window where she picks up her coffee mug. It's cold now, but she gulps at the thick black liquid anyway as she stares at the green curtain.

*

As Rose walks down her own street she thinks about Bronwyn's cold words and wonders when her friend became so jaded. When they were teenagers Bronwyn used to be a firecracker. She was loud and defended her friends and family with a warrior-like stance. She fought and laughed and danced and drank. Now she has faded away into nothingness. *She's like me*, thinks Rose, *quiet and subdued and unhappy.* And the encounter in Bronwyn's kitchen has almost made her forget about the previous night's trauma, until she walks past the Parkenson house. From the corner of her eye she sees Mrs Parkenson in her garden. Rose slows down and is about to nod a greeting when suddenly a great gob of spit lands on her shoe. It is Mrs Parkenson's teenage son, she hadn't seen him at first as he's standing by the fence. Rose's mouth falls open and she looks wildly around, noticing now that everyone is outside. All of their neighbours are hanging around the gates, watching her do the walk of shame.

And she doesn't know how to react, this is something totally new. Raised single-handedly by a mother who ruled with a rod of steel, she's spent her whole life playing by the rules. Never had she given her mother a moment of trouble or worry and, unlike Bronwyn, she had never shoplifted, skipped school or been in trouble with the law. She had never given anyone cause to chastise her. Until now.

"Traitor!" shouted someone and the yell is like a starting pistol.

Now her mother is coming at her, out of her own gate five doors away and Rose feels her face go cold but there's a fascination there too, just how much Rose's own mother, Kathleen, is holding the same sort of fury that Mary Dean had earlier. Kathleen doesn't share the physical similarities of Mary. Where Mary is tall and stately, Kathleen is slight, but she's moving at a speed that Rose has never seen before and then she's there, in front of Rose and Kathleen's hand shoots out, grips her daughter's arm and in one fluid movement, she's pulled down the path and into the house.

Kathleen slams the door shut and turns to face her daughter.

"Mam—"

Kathleen slaps Rose's face. Hard. "How could you?" Kathleen's face is ablaze with fury. "Why couldn't you stick to your own?"

Rose flinches at her mother's wrath and tried to summon Bronwyn in her head. When she's in a bind she always thinks of what Bronwyn would do. Bronwyn would just tell Kathleen to fuck off.

"He's just a friend," Rose whispers.

"That's a lie!" Kathleen roars as Rose begins to shake. She doesn't know how to placate her mother, she never has. She can never reach her.

"Mam...," Rose is openly crying.

"A Protestant pig! My daughter and a pig. I'm a laughing stock! My neighbours, who always respected me, are laughing at me!" Kathleen shouts.

They never respected you, they think you're a witch. When I was a child the other kids dared each other to knock on this very door and outrun the witch. But Rose doesn't say that aloud. She has never stood up to Kathleen, but she wants her mother to try and understand what danger she had been in last night.

"They left him on the ground and came after me. I had to run away, I had to hide because I was so frightened and I was all alone out there. I could have been shot or raped...," she tails off, knowing her words won't have made an impact anyway.

There's no love here, she thinks, nothing like Mary's love for her son. Why is that? Why does my mother care about what the neighbours think instead of caring about me?

Kathleen's face is ashen and Rose frowns. "I don't know what to do, mam."

Her mother's movements are slow now, not jerky and fast. It's as if the rage has left her and in its place is nothing. Kathleen reaches past Rose and opens the front door.

Rose glances out at the people still holding court in the street. What's she supposed to do? Leave? What is Kathleen asking of her? And her mother isn't even looking at her anymore, she's fixed her empty stare on a spot on the wall.

Rose slips out of the door and it closes softly in her face.

The crowd shift behind her. They are quiet too, perhaps sensing the unease. Rose walks down the path. The fear and her tears have gone. She doesn't know what just happened. She doesn't know what to do. And she's fast running out of people to go to.

*

Bronwyn is still in the kitchen when Dan comes down. She automatically glances at the clock. It's early, for him, anyway. He moves past her without speaking and goes out into the garden. She watches from the window. The shed door is swinging open and he slams it closed, props a brick in front of it to keep it shut.

"Rose's man was shot last night," she says, when he comes back into the kitchen.

Dan, bare-chested, opens the fridge. The contents have not changed since the day before and he slams it closed.

"Did you hear me?" she asks.

He mumbles, rubs at his head and reaches for his rolling tobacco on the side.

"Fucking kids," he mutters.

"What?"

Deftly he rolls a cigarette and opens the back door again. A rush of cold air comes in and she shivers.

"Can't you hear them?"

She hadn't, but now she does. They are playing two doors down. She imagines them bundled up in thick winter clothes, chasing around the garden. They are young, no more than toddlers, really. Their mother, Sue, seems to pop one out every year.

"They're just playing," she replies. "Did you hear about Rose?"

He shakes his head, lights the fag and sucks on it.

"Her boyfriend got shot."

"Who the fuck is her boyfriend?"

His interest is piqued now and his attention is so unfamiliar that for a moment she doesn't know how to continue.

"Connor... some lad, protestant, obviously." She stops talking, watches him through narrowed eyes as he flicks his ash outside the door.

Suddenly she needs to get out. The kitchen is stifling now, though moments earlier she had felt the cold blast of winter and she pushes back her chair sharply and stands up.

"I'm going out," she says.

He has moved outside now, and she sees his hand rise in a dismissive gesture, or maybe he's just flicking his cigarette.

She's breathless as she pulls her coat on, puts her keys and purse in her pocket and slams the front door behind her. She waits until she hears the slam of the back door that tells her he has retreated back into the house before making her way up the side of the house. She shoves the brick out of the way with her foot and pulls the shed door open. In the dusty gloom she can make out shapes stacked up neatly against the far wall. Pinching her lips together she nods, once to herself, before quietly closing the door and putting the brick back in its place.

Images of last night's clothes, balled up and discarded in the bathroom wash over her. Dan in front of the mirror, naked, touching himself, visibly aroused. Shaking her head as if to dispel the thoughts, she hurries back down the alley and across the street to the telephone box on the corner. With shaking fingers she digs a coin out of her pocket and rings Rose's home and Kathleen answers, short and sharp, and Bronwyn groans inwardly.

"Hi, Mrs James, is Rose there?"

Someone is breathing shallowly on the other end but nobody speaks. Bronwyn is about to repeat herself when there is a click and a dialing tone in her ear as Kathleen hangs up.

Well, Rose must have told her all about Connor. But, where had she gone? In times of trouble the two girls always went to each other, but obviously Rose hadn't come back to her.

Maybe she has gone back to the hospital. She hangs up the receiver and taps her fingernails on the phone. She opens the door of the phone box, looks up and down the street before retreating back inside. She digs around in her pocket, slips another coin in and dials a number before she can change her mind. A nameless, faceless, bored sounding man answers at the other end. Bronwyn talks quickly, spilling out her words fast so she can't change her mind. The man is speaking at the other end, asking questions, but she's said enough. She hangs up and as she backs out of the telephone box, Bronwyn sees a bus turning the corner at the top of the road. She steps off the kerb and flags it down.

*

At the hospital, Rose sits in the waiting room. Mary is there, accusing in her silence. When she can no longer bear it she speaks up.

"What happened to Connor's dad?"

Mary glances at her but says nothing.

"I need to know what to expect, my mother... I think she kicked me out." Rose says haltingly. "I mean, I know what to expect, obviously, after last night. But, will you tell me?"

Mary's face is so taught and pale that Rose thinks she might slap her, just like her own mother did. But to her surprise, Mary answers. Her words are faltering, halted, heartfelt.

"I can't... they got him. Like they got Connor," Mary swallows loudly and shoots a look at Rose. "I can't tell you much more, do you understand, girl, that I don't think about that night?"

Rose nods her understanding, but after a pause Mary continues talking.

"They got him, they used a gun and a bullet, just like with my boy. And if they'd have stopped there he would still be here today." Mary stops, gulps in air and finishes in a rush. "But they didn't."

It soon becomes apparent that Mary is not going to say anymore, so Rose stands up.

"More coffee?" she asks.

"Yes."

"Does Connor know? I mean, have you ever told him the whole story?" asks Rose as she retrieved two more coffees.

"He knows everything. I never keep anything from him." Her voice is full of pride, boastful that she is so close to her son.

But he doesn't tell you everything, thinks Rose spitefully, *he didn't tell you about me.*

A nurse comes in and casts a glance at Rose before turning to Mary.

"Mrs Dean, your son is awake and asking for you."

Mary nods and sweeps out of the door. Rose, still at the coffee machine, puts the drinks aside and runs after her.

*

"Hey!" Connor's eyes are wide and anxious as Mary strides into his room with Rose following close behind her. "You two..."

Mary reaches him first, hugging Connor before standing back. Rose moves forward, crying already. Relief that he's not dead, not like his poor dad.

"It's okay. I'm all right, see?" Connor grips her hand. He shows them his leg, tells that how the doctor said he was lucky, it was clean, no bones damaged. The shot was off, just a flesh wound.

Despite the good news on his leg he looks awful. His right eye is swollen closed, and he has stitches in his forehead, where he had received a vicious cut. Rose sits on the edge of the bed, taking care not to touch his bandaged leg.

"Girl's been kicked out of her home," announces Mary.

Connor looks horrified. "Does everyone know?"

"Yes," Mary replies, and at his expression, "what did you expect?"

"What are you going to do?" he questions Rose.

There is a lull in conversation so awkward that Rose thinks she may start crying again. The silence stretches into minutes and Rose is just about to say that she will stay with Bronwyn, when Connor turns to his mother. With a look that Rose can't quite decipher he says, "She'll have to stay at ours."

Rose doesn't want to look at Mary, but she does. She wishes she hadn't.

Chapter 5

The curtain moves, three pairs of eyes look up, no doubt in relief that someone else is there to help the awkward conversation.

"Bronwyn!" Rose cries and stands up to greet her friend. Relief that she is there, a fourth person who will fill the hateful silences.

"Bronwyn, hey?" Connor smiles in her direction. "Rose's friend?"

Bronwyn studies the boy in the bed. He's nothing like she expected. How did Rose land this one being as plain as she is? She hates herself immediately for the thought but she can't ignore it. He's quite dark skinned, his hair is as dark as hers and he is extremely good looking; dark eyes and chiselled, classically handsome features. He seems an awful lot younger than Rose though, something her friend had not mentioned.

"I'm sorry it's under these circumstances that we finally meet," says Bronwyn and then turns to Mary. "Hello. Are you Connor's ma?"

"That I am," she replies and stands up. "I'll wait outside."

"What's her problem?" asks Bronwyn, once Mary has left.

"Bron, I need to ask a favour," says Rose in a small voice, dismissing Bronwyn's question about Mary's sudden departure. "I need some things, I'm staying at Connor's, my mum…" She tails off. "I don't know what happened; she hit me though. I don't think I can go home."

"You're staying at Connor's?" Bronwyn looks between them. "Is that a good idea?"

Rose and Connor shrug simultaneously, and Bronwyn shakes her head. Do they not know that it was their relationship that got Connor shot in the first place? Neither of them deigns to answer her. "I'll get your stuff and bring it round to Connor's. You just write me the address and it'll be there." She waits while Rose finds a pen and an old envelope in her bag. As her friend prints the address in her neat, careful handwriting, Bronwyn is aware of Connor's gaze. She looks up, once, in his direction, but quickly glances away when he smiles at her. There is intensity in his smile, just like how Danny used to smile at her, once upon a time. It's not how her best friend's boyfriend should look at her.

Rose has finished writing and now she is looking at them, flicking her gaze between the two of them. She hands the address over and shifts on the bed, taking Connor's hand in hers and fixing a stare on Bronwyn. The atmosphere changes, suddenly and noticeably. *Is she warning me?* Wonders Bronwyn. All of their lives it was Bronwyn with the boys, before Danny. This is a side of Rose that Bronwyn is not familiar with. She says nothing, takes the paper off Rose and stuffs it in her pocket. She stands, ready to leave, uncomfortable in the charade of Rose claiming her man.

*

It doesn't take Bronwyn long to get to Rose's house. She's known Kathleen James all of her life, and can easily see why Rose is so scared of her mother. There's is the neatest house on the street. The windows are always gleaming, in fact throughout her childhood Bronwyn always associated the smell of white vinegar with Kathleen. There is never any bird shit on these windows, and the step is cleaned with bleach and a scrubbing brush every day. She raps on the door and as she waits she spies a single weed growing up through a crack in the path. It gives her a sad sort of pleasure, to see the one that Kathleen has missed.

"I might have known she'd send you," says Kathleen as she opens the door.

Bronwyn thinks of the earlier phone call she made and how Kathleen hung up, and with that in mind she pushes her way into the house and immediately heads upstairs to Rose's room.

"I'm here for her things. I won't be long," she calls over her shoulder.

As she enters Rose's room, Kathleen is right behind her.

"You can't just barge in here like this!"

"I can, and I have. I'm not Rose. I'm not frightened of you," says Bronwyn, and pulls Rose's suitcase off the top of her wardrobe.

Kathleen backs off to the doorway, her mouth twisted with bitterness. Bronwyn works methodically, determined not to rush. When she turns to gather some clothes out of Rose's chest of drawers, Kathleen has gone.

Bronwyn packs the last of Rose's clothes and walks back down the stairs. Kathleen is at the bottom, standing in front of the door. Bronwyn keeps right on moving until Kathleen has no choice but to move aside. Bronwyn pauses at the front door and turns back to face Kathleen.

"I met Connor tonight. He's a nice lad, a good lad, and it'd be a shame for you to fall out with Rose over this."

Kathleen clenches her fists. "Don't you give me advice on family matters!" she hisses. "Not you! Don't you dare."

"She's your daughter; you should be helping her, not kicking her out." Bronwyn opens the door and shoves the suitcase out in front of her. "You've never loved Rose, the poor cow. You act as though you don't even like her!"

She stalks down the road, dragging the suitcase behind her. She knows Kathleen's story, she's not supposed to but in Newry it seems to be an open secret, one that everyone knows but only ever discusses in hushed whispers, and never in front of Kathleen or Rose. She would even go so far as to say she can understand why Kathleen is so bitter and twisted, but it's not Rose's fault. A cluster of British soldiers stand smoking on the corner of Kathleen's street. They watch her pass, whisper something and then shout an obscenity. She raises her middle finger over her shoulder and their laughter follows her.

As she turns into Kidds Road a police car overtakes her, swiftly followed by a second. Making a conscious effort not to break into a run she walks up to the telephone box in which she stood earlier, standing behind it as two officers get out of the first car and walk up to her house. There are two more men in the second car and they remain inside. Bronwyn stands motionless, watching the men as they converse briefly. The taller of the two heads to the front door while the other makes his way up the alley at the side of the house.

Bronwyn covers her mouth and bites at her knuckles as the door is opened. Her mother stands there and though Bronwyn can't hear what she is saying, Alia begins to gesture. Calmly, the officer moves her aside and makes his way into the house. The door closes behind him and picking up the suitcase, hoping the two men still in the police car don't see her, Bronwyn walks as quickly as she can down the road.

Two streets away she stops, drops the case to the ground and sits atop it. Where is she going to go? To see Rose, to explain to her what Danny has done? No, now is not the time and besides when she explains she wants Connor to be there too. She continues walking the streets until she is too cold to be outside and finally, an hour after she left the shadow of the phone box she reckons its safe enough to head back home.

The front door is ajar when she arrives and the doorframe is splintered. She doesn't know why, when she was watching from her hiding place, her mother had opened the door and the officers had gone inside.

Bronwyn's mother comes down the hall. "Oh, Jesus Christ, Bronwyn, they've taken Dan!"

Bronwyn pulls off her scarf and hangs it on the banister. Her mother, Alia, is fraught. Bronwyn doesn't know why, she doesn't like Dan any more than anyone else.

Bronwyn pauses, unsure of how to act. "What for?" she asks, eventually, wondering if it is the question she should be asking.

"It all happened so quickly," Alia says, wringing her hands. "Dan tried to run but there were more of them in the garden, they took him away."

"What happened to the door?" Bronwyn glances back at the splintered frame.

"He fought them when they took him out. Danny kicked it, I think."

Bronwyn's eyes fill with tears and she balls her fists and rubs her face. Alia pulls her against her. "Don't worry, we'll get him out," she whispers.

Bronwyn pulls away and shakes her head. "I'm not upset about Dan!" She looks at the broken frame, one more thing in this house that looks like shite because of him. Now it's an eyesore, just like the garden. She stomps into the kitchen, pulls up short. There's a chair upturned in the middle of the room, is it the one that Danny was sitting in when they came for him? She shoves it hard and goes to the window.

Her mother follows her in and Bronwyn turns around to look at her. She looks good, her mother. She's slim and athletic, her hair, black like Bronwyn's, is sleek and cut in a fashionable bob. Bronwyn's father has never been around so Alia has never been worn down and worn out by a man. As she looks at her mother she has a sudden pang of regret about leaving home. Silly, really, she's not lived with her mother for ten years.

"I know the police have arrested him," she says and adds defiantly, "I called them. I got him arrested."

She expects an outburst, but her mother just looks at her strangely, like she doesn't believe her.

"He deserved it, I don't regret it," Bronwyn snaps, to break the silence.

"Do you want to tell me about it?"

"Not really, no." She shakes her head, feeling tears welling up again. "I'll have to get someone in to fix the door."

"Forget about the bloody door, we'll sort it out later. Did he do something, to you I mean?" Alia's dark eyes flash and Bronwyn sees herself, her old self in that expression. She needs to get back to her old self. She doesn't know where the old Bronwyn went, or even really why she left. It's that thing of being worn down again, the months and the years and the secrets, the loneliness so big like a chasm and the ever widening gap just take their toll.

"No, not me," she raises her voice over the noise of the kettle that she's switched on. "Ma, do you want to stay here tonight?" She doesn't know why she asked that, she never asks anything of her mother.

Alia nods and steers Bronwyn to the chair. "I'll make the tea," she says softly.

*

Later, to avoid Alia's questions which started coming thick and fast, Bronwyn takes Rose's things over to Connor's house. She pulls the case along, her nerves jangling as she moves further away from home into territory that she really shouldn't be headed for. The streets look the same as hers, as do the houses. Shingle fronted homes interspersed with almost pretty white fronted terraces. The demographic here is mostly Irish Catholics, Connor and his mother are in a very small minority. She wonders if they suffer for that, if their home is graffitied and bottles of piss are thrown at their windows. She doesn't pass anyone on the route, not even a lone dog walker. There are butterflies in her stomach and she knows they are not only because of where she is walking, but what she will do when she reaches her destination. Does she tell them what she's done? Or wait, and tell Connor himself? She really wants to tell Connor that she got her husband arrested, she wants to see what he will say but she has no idea why. She doesn't want to impress him, does she? He's not hers to impress, is he? She has no answers to the questions that she is asking herself when she arrives and she stops outside on the pavement. Studying the house she can see that Mary has tried to make it nice. It's a council place, they almost all are, but there is evidence of maintenance and care. *It is like Kathleen's house*, she thinks, shuddering. Thin green shoots are poking out of the frost covered ground under the window. Next month there will be daffodils here, all in a neat row. The window frames are painted a mahogany brown, no peeling white paint here, not like Bronwyn's own house.

It takes her a while before she realizes that Mary Dean is standing on her doorstep, watching Bronwyn with a cool gaze.

"Hello, Mrs Dean, how are you?" She asks, pulling the suitcase up to the house. "Have they let Connor out?"

Mary stands aside to let her in. "No, tomorrow, hopefully." She looks down at the suitcase, glances up and down the streets before stepping back, reluctantly it seems to Bronwyn, and opens the door wider.

She doesn't smile, Mary, Bronwyn notices. Her face is pinched and pale but Bronwyn can't blame her. She knows what it will be like for Mary, Rose and Connor. Their lives are about to become very difficult.

The suitcase gets caught on the step and by the time Bronwyn has yanked it free and dragged it into the narrow hallway, Mary is nowhere to be seen. So she won't tell them about Danny then, not today. Disappointment pits in her stomach but she doesn't know why, it should be a relief that she gets a reprieve.

Bronwyn walks through, looks left into an empty lounge. Straight ahead she sees the kitchen and it is here that she locates Rose, sitting as straight as a statue, her hands wrapped around a glass.

"I got your stuff," says Bronwyn, and when Rose doesn't reply she stands the case in the corner and sits down opposite her friend. "Are you okay?"

Rose looks up at that. She doesn't answer, but there's an expression in her eyes that Bronwyn has never seen before. It's not fear; she's seen that on Rose plenty of times. It's not anger or hurt. She can't pinpoint it.

Bronwyn leans back and looks around the kitchen. The beige Formica worktops are clean and neat and the brown carpet looks quite new. There's a sideboard in the corner, crammed with a couple of dozen or so photographs. They are all of Connor.

It seems like there has never been anyone else in Mary's life, not for the last however many years. Which reminds her, "how old *is* Connor?"

"Twenty-three," replies Rose, blushing now.

"Fecking cradle snatcher." Bronwyn nudges her, trying for laughter, but when her gaze lands on the photographs again her smile fades.

All Mary has had and all she's got is Connor.

Bronwyn inhales sharply. "Do they have other family, grandparents, or nieces or nephews?"

Rose shrugs and turns slowly to look at the photos behind her. "I don't think so, Connor's never mentioned anyone except his mother."

Bronwyn breathes out and turns away from the sideboard. Where will Rose fit in here? Will Mary make space for her? She thinks of Mary's face, sharp and bitter.

Chapter 6

February 1981

I can't believe I've been arrested. Fucking arrested! The police came to the house, barged their way in and dragged me out. Bronwyn's fucking mother was there, hanging about as usual, wringing her hands as I tried to get the pigs off me.

"What shall I do?" She was calling as they dragged me down the path, in full view of the neighbours, giving them a bloody good show.

They want to talk to me about Connor Dean, amongst other things. I won't speak to them, I won't answer their questions. This is nothing to do with them. This is work, the shooting was work, and it's got fuck all to do with the police.

They put me in a cell and I sit there for hours. They bring me food eventually and I spit on it. They take it away.

They bring me another tray later and I go even further; I piss on it and up the door too. The guard takes the tray away, disgust written clearly on his face.

They bring me back to the small, airless room and I lean back in my chair, rocking on the back legs as if I'm still in school.

I've not been arrested before but I know the drill. I can play these people.

There are two men, detectives, firing questions. There's no good cop, bad cop, these two are both bad.

I say nothing.

As they talk I wonder what Bronwyn is doing. Her mother would have told her by now. I almost wish Bron had been home when the police came knocking. She'd have given them her attitude. The old Bronwyn would have come back, the fiery, feisty girl I used to know.

She'll be here soon, and I'll know when she arrives, I'll hear her. She'll have found a solicitor from somewhere, she'll make them come here and let me out.

Sometimes we don't see eye to eye. She nags, but we've been together years, we've been married for a decade, of course she's going to nag.

Women do. But that's what they are there for. We go out and sort out all the shite. The woman looks after everything else. They're good at it.

I smirk at the policemen and they look wrong-footed for a moment.

I recall the shed and everything that they would have taken away. For a moment my smile almost wavers until I remember, where I'm going, I won't need any weapons.

I'll be my own weapon, and I'm more powerful than any firearm.

*

When Rose woke she expected to be disorientated. She's slept in the same bedroom for thirty years, but even before she opened her eyes she remembered everything. She thinks she's been dreaming about it all night, which is why it's so fresh in her mind this morning.

She's in the box room, not Connor's bedroom, not in his bed, which to Rose seems a little callous of Mary, though not unexpected. In fact, she can't believe she is here at all.

Mary.

She hadn't spoken to Rose at all yesterday, apart from when she showed her where she would be sleeping and where the bathroom was. An atmosphere hangs heavy over the Dean household, and Rose can't wait for Connor to come home.

She folds back the covers and pads over to the window. Opening it, she leans out, ignoring the cold as she looks up and down the street. The view is not much different to that from her own bedroom window; row upon row of terrace houses, broken up by a few muddy fields. Streets that she knows so well already from sneaking around here the last six months.

She wonders what her mother is doing this morning. Did she continue last night with her normal routine, dinner at six o'clock and bed straight after the ten o'clock news? Or did she forgo her tea last night and crack open a bottle of gin instead? Did she drink herself stupid, crying over her behaviour towards her only child?

She hears the faint sound of a radio coming from below as a downstairs window is opened and Mary sticks her head out and glances left and right before lighting up a cigarette. The smoke drifts slowly up towards Rose.

"Good morning," she says.

Her voice is too quiet, Mary doesn't hear her.

Rose clears her throat, closes the window softly, and crawls back into bed.

*

Mary Dean slams the kitchen window shut and smokes the rest of her cigarette inside. She heard the mouse saying good morning, but she's still too angry to talk in a civilised manner to the girl. And she's furious with Connor. Of all the people who should have known better. She sinks into a chair at the kitchen table. His father, her lover, her one, single, love of a lifetime had been killed in exactly the same situation. Connor has been so selfish, showing no regard for her feelings or the memories that this whole thing is bringing up.

She lets out a hiss between her teeth as the cigarette burns down to her knuckles. The flare of pain doubles her anger and she roughly stubs it out in the ashtray.

The girl, Mary can't warm to her, can't even bring herself to try, but she is living under her roof. And she can't throw her out because Connor will go with her.

Soon enough she hears the tell-tale squeak of springs as the girl gets back into bed. Lazy little bitch, does she not work? Is Mary expected to clothe and feed her? Connor doesn't earn enough to take care of her.

Mary stifles a scream, wishes she had a close friend or some family to escape to. But Mary's never had anybody, only Connor.

She can't lose him, he's the only one left.

She won't let him be taken away, especially not by a little nobody like Rose, not while she's still got breath left in her body.

*

As Bronwyn boils the kettle for her morning coffee she stares around the kitchen. This is her room, her sanctuary. Like so many women all over the world the kitchen is her heart of the home and she wonders if she should maybe attempt to paint it while Danny is away. She considers her options, maybe a pale green to match her makeshift curtain.

That curtain. Abandoning thoughts of colour schemes she moves over to the window and yanks the material aside. The view of the garden draws a sharp breath, the concrete, unevenly poured, lumpy and just an eyesore. She can't do anything about that, but perhaps she could put some pots around the garden. She remembers the bulbs outside Mary's house that she saw last night. It's not too late for daffodils or crocus plants.

It's a sense of hope, but it's a feeling so unfamiliar that it vanishes in an instant. Bronwyn pulls the curtain back across and goes to the fridge. She reaches for the milk but pauses as she sees Dan's Pilsner cans at the back. She plucks one out, slams the fridge door and sits down at the kitchen table. The kettle clicks off as it boils, but instead of pouring her coffee she pulls the tab off the tin of beer. It froths up and she picks it up, sups the white foam away and then gulps from the can. When she's finished, she crumples it in her fist and retrieves the second from the fridge.

Her mother is still asleep when she takes the third beer into the garden. She can see her breath puffing out in front of her as she makes her way across the concrete and down towards the railway track at the bottom. Belatedly she realises she's only wearing her thin pyjamas, so she slugs at the beer. It works a little; she's not as cold as she should be.

She likes it down here by the railway line. There is a lovely large flat rock that she sits on. It's her chair and there's a smaller one beside it which she uses to put her drink on. The commuter train passes many, many times a day, going all the way to Belfast and back again. When they had moved here to the house in Kidds Road, Bronwyn had been concerned about the noise from the trains. Now, the sound of the railway and the slight vibration that can be felt in the house is a comfort. It's green down here too, if she sits with her back to the garden, which she invariably does, she can look out over the meadows and ignore the concrete jungle behind her.

Sometimes the train will stop just before the bridge and she gets to watch the passengers on board. She imagines where they are travelling to, or from. Sometimes her thoughts go deeper, like the time she saw the woman staring out of the window who looked like she was crying. That made her sit up, the vision of the lady around her own age. Why the tears? Is she scared because she has broken away and is heading off on her own? Or is she sad because she can't break free, and she's on her way home to the same old life and the same old hurt, never with any means of escape?

She hears the slap of approaching footsteps and she turns to see her mother, fully dressed with her hair done and her makeup on, picking her way to the railway track.

"Christ, what are you doing out here?" Her mother asks as she stands over Bronwyn, looking around, presumably for somewhere to sit.

Bronwyn attempts to conceal the beer can by shifting in front of it, but it's too late.

"It's not even 8 o'clock," says Alia.

"I'd had two cans by seven," replies Bronwyn and looks away over the fields.

But Alia's attention has been captured by something else and she stares down at Bronwyn's pyjamas. Bronwyn, not liking the scrutiny, tries to cover her chest by folding her arms. Alia's mouth is working now, and she crouches down beside her daughter.

"Come inside, with me, darling," she says as she bites her lip and breathes out. "You're bleeding…"

Bronwyn looks down at herself. Now she's been told she can feel it, wet and warm against her body. There's been a cramping in her stomach all night, but the alcohol had deadened it and she had forgotten. She allows Alia to help her up and as she stands, a lot more blood flows out of her.

"It's… I don't think it's my period," Bronwyn says and she can feel hot tears in her eyes as she doubles over with the sudden pain.

Chapter 7

She had dropped her purse in Kilmorey Park. That was how they first met, Rose and Connor. She had taken a lunch break at the office where she worked as a copy typist in Cowan Street, and the day was so hot and sunny that she just had to get outside. It was nearing the end of August, who knew how many other nice days there would be?

She bought a coke and a slice of sponge cake from the stall in the park and as she turned away she spotted a bench being vacated by an elderly couple. All of the other seats were full, so she slid her purse in her handbag and hurried across the grass. She had just sat down and taken her first bite of the cake when she noticed a man jogging towards her. She didn't want company, hoped that he wasn't going to ask to share her bench, so she looked off into the distance as his shadow fell over her.

"You dropped this," he said.

She looked up then, saw her red purse in his hand. She looked at him, at his face, and felt something new in her stomach. She attempted to smile, and then chewed for what seemed like forever to get rid of the mouthful of cake.

Somehow he ended up sitting down and somehow, to her surprise, they talked. It wasn't her usual sort of conversation, where she would nod and insert the occasional 'hmm'. She actually conversed with him. She felt a part of it, and her shy and introverted nature melted away. She studied him, coming to the conclusion that he was young, a lot younger than her, barely out of his teens or just in his early twenties, she would say.

Though their chat was easy, it seemed impossible to ask to see him again, so when the time came for her to go back to work, she gave him a half wave. She paused, too long, in case *he* asked to see *her*, and when he didn't, she hurried away, embarrassed.

She couldn't help but go back the next day, just in case. She took extra care with her appearance, brushing her hair in the loo at work, carefully applying a little bit of extra mascara and lipstick. She had stared at herself in the mirror, worried that she had jinxed it by trying so hard, so she messed up her hair a little and scrubbed her face clean.

It worked. He came. He looked surprised to see her but she wondered if maybe he had had the same thoughts as her. She told herself not to be so stupid. It was her who had been a stranger to the park the day before, he probably came every day. He had tickets to see a comedian at the Daisy Hill Social Club, would she like to go, this Friday night?

She had made a funny noise in the back of her throat and she had blushed, hoping that he hadn't heard it. Yes, she would. And so Friday night saw them at the club. It was dark inside, and though the comedian had been funny, she didn't laugh that much. Neither did he and in the intermission they had ducked outside. It was a warm night, but she shivered when he led her around the back of the club house and pushed her up against the wall. She couldn't believe they were going to do it here, outside, where anyone could walk past. And as he lifted her skirt and moved her legs apart with his knees she clung onto his shoulders and looked around. Then, the sweetness overcame her, and she didn't care who walked by as she gasped and gripped him tight.

Now, she's got what she wanted for so long; to see his home and meet his mother. But now she's got what she wants, now she's sitting in Mary Dean's house, it doesn't feel how she expected it to.

*

By the time Bronwyn arrived at the hospital there was nothing left. She lay still as she was examined, endured a D&C to ensure everything had gone. They advised her to take painkillers but she doesn't want them. She wants to feel this. This is the most she has felt in months.

She asks to go home, and the doctor agrees as long as someone is there. Alia immediately reassures Bronwyn that she will stay again tonight.

Now they are home and all Bronwyn wants is for Alia to go and leave her be.

"Please, ma, I just want to sleep," Bronwyn implores.

"You can sleep while I'm here," says Alia as she puts the kettle on. "I can't leave you on your own."

Bronwyn grips the edge of the table and looks towards the garden. She wants to scream, but if she loses her temper Alia will never go. She edges towards the door and slips her feet into her slippers.

"Where are you going now?" Alia abandons the tea making and makes for Bronwyn.

"Just down the garden, just for some air."

Bronwyn slips out and pulls her cardigan tighter around her as she trudges across the concrete and heads to the tracks. It's getting dark now, she's spent all day in the lousy hospital and she doesn't want to lose the light. If she does, she'll have to wait until tomorrow.

When she reaches her rock she casts a glance behind her to make sure Alia hasn't followed her. When she is sure that she is alone she kneels down in the wet grass. There it is, the remains of her pregnancy, just a bloodstain with a jellied texture. A stain on a rock, soon to be washed away by the harsh February rains. Suddenly it's very important that that doesn't happen. She stands up, brushes off her knees and moves down to the railway track. She picks up a large piece of flint and, back on her knees beside her rock, she scrapes some of the hard earth away. She pulls up a fistful of grass and scoops up as much of the red matter that she can before laying it in the small hole she has made. She covers it over, retrieves some of the peach coloured stones from the other side of the track and puts them on top of the tiny grave. She leans back on her heels and looks at her hands. They are covered with soil and blood, and she puts them to her face and lets her tears mingle with the stains.

*

Alia pulls the horrible old curtain aside and looks out down the garden. She holds onto the green material and decides to buy Bronwyn a nice blind, maybe those fancy horizontal ones, they do them in a nice wood effect. It will be expensive and she's heard they are a pain to dust and keep clean, but she wants to do something for her daughter.

Because that's her problem right now, the feeling of being useless. Bronwyn is sinking, spiralling down in a pit filled with despair and she's so closed off, so private and so close to the edge, that Alia doesn't feel that she can ask too much. All she can do is keep on brewing the tea and making sure that Bronwyn eats and sleeps.

Alia lets the curtain fall and steps outside the back door. She can hear the door of the shed banging and she makes her way over to it. She's surprised the outbuilding is still standing. It's as old as the house and the wooden structure is weather beaten and unstable.

She pushes the door and sees that it won't close; it's actually dropped on the hinges. She opens it and peers in. It is empty, but she knows it wasn't bare when the police came. They removed everything, covered in blankets and stacked in boxes. She thinks back to the covered shapes, she hadn't taken much notice at the time, too concerned about them dragging Danny out of the house, but now she thinks about it, it makes sense. The odd hours that Danny keeps, his secretive nature, the absence of friends and finally, the fact that he's now in prison.

She hears something moving outside and she hoists the door and slams it closed with more force than is necessary.

Bronwyn is sloping past on the other side of the garden. Alia bites her lip, looks once more at the shed, and follows her daughter into the house.

*

Rose awoke to her second morning in the Dean house late. She had watched the hours of the night before tick past, counting them off one by one by the fluorescent hands of the clock. It was getting near daybreak when she must have finally nodded off, and now it is ten o'clock.

Mary will think she is so dreadfully lazy.

Then a second thought strikes her and she sits bolt upright in the single bed. Connor is coming home today! She dresses quickly, pulling a pair of jeans and a thick jumper from the still unpacked case that Bronwyn had bought round. She drags a brush through her hair and ties it back before hurrying down the stairs.

The house is quiet, no radio on, no television. Rose walks through the hallway, looking in at the lounge and the kitchen. The house is empty. Mary has left to collect Connor without her.

A blinding panic builds in her and she stands in the kitchen. She is alone and even when Connor gets here she's still going to be alone. Mary is going to freeze her out, she's already started. She doesn't want a Catholic woman taking away her precious son because Connor is all that Mary has.

She looks at the photographs on the sideboard, all of Connor, marking every year of his life so far. She sees now what Bronwyn had been asking the other night. Where is everyone else, the grandparents or the friends or the cousins? There is nobody else in Mary's life, and really she is no different to Rose's mother. They are both angry, bitter women, twisted in their loneliness. Nobody else has telephoned this house or called round. Mary obviously does not encourage friendships. Rose wonders if her neighbours know anything about her and Connor. Do they think this is a Catholic family? Do they even notice Mary at all? They noticed all right the other night, when Connor lay on the cobbles bleeding from a gunshot wound. She recalls them crowding around the ambulance, but she doesn't remember any of the people offering Mary a kind gesture or a word of comfort.

And if this is the way of the world, and it's not just Rose's mother who is standoffish and cold, but it is actually a common occurrence, should she attempt reconciliation with her own mother? She's never been apart from Kathleen, not really. Has she stayed away long enough to have frightened her mother? If she goes back home, right now, would she finally be greeted with open arms? Because she's just coming to realise, that apart from Bronwyn and Connor, she really doesn't have anyone else looking out for her. Pulling on her coat, she leaves the house and makes her way across town.

There's a strange smell emanating from inside her mother's house, something sour and rotten. And as she lets herself in and stands in the hallway she wonders if it always carried this scent. She tried over the years to spend as little time as possible here. Throughout her childhood and youth she was always at Bronwyn's where, although they had little money, Alia always managed to put a hot meal on the table at least once a day. There were only the two of them there, Bronwyn and her mother, and Rose spent those years in a warm fold, punctured only occasionally by stabs of jealousy. When the two friends got older and Bronwyn started going out with Danny, she tagged along with them sometimes, but Dan always made her a bit uncomfortable. She knew that he wanted Bronwyn to himself, and when he changed tact and got a bit over friendly, Rose stopped spending so much time in their company and began hiding out at the library. The library was okay. It was clean and tidy and she could lose an entire afternoon in there. And the library didn't smell funny, not like this house. And it's something else, this odour, it wasn't always as bad as this. She nudges open the door to the living room. Kathleen is curled in a corner of the sofa, swaddled in a thick blanket. She is asleep and Rose sees the tell-tale almost empty bottle of gin on the carpet.

Rose backs out of the room and closes the door quietly.

There's nothing for her here.

*

Connor is dressed and practicing on his crutches when Mary arrives to collect him. An odd look flits across his face when he sees that she is alone. Mary tilts her head to the side and studies him hard. Is he hopeful that the girl has gone for good? Or disappointed that Mary has come on her own?

"The girl's at home, love," she says. "She's still in bed by all accounts."

He glances at the clock, frowning, and Mary bites her lip against the words that she wants to say. That if Connor was her man she'd have damn well been here even if she hadn't slept for two days straight. She can't ostracise Connor though. She's lucky he's still at home, most men his age are married by now but she's enjoyed him being close, if he moved out… It doesn't bear thinking about. But the girl can't stay at their house forever, either. She couldn't stand the thought of sharing her home indefinitely with her, and on a separate note, the longer she stays the more dangerous it becomes for all three of them. But if she brings this up and the girl moves out, Connor might follow her. And they couldn't rent a house in Newry, or indeed even Northern Ireland in general. They would have to move away, far away, and then she would have lost the only thing she cares about in her life.

Mary puffs her cheeks out. She's going to have to handle this very carefully, and she's going to have to try and get rid of the damn girl.

"Ready?" she asks him, painting on a smile.

"Yes, let's go," he replies, and walking slowly side by side, they make their way out of the hospital.

"Do you like her, then?" he asks as they wait in the taxi rank.

Mary shrugs. "I've not really seen her to form an opinion, I showed her to her bedroom and she's pretty much stayed there. I cooked a nice lamb dinner last night but she wasn't interested."

It's a lie that she hopes doesn't get her found out. She did cook a lamb dinner, but it was just some chops for herself. If Connor asks Rose about it, Mary will just say that she called up the stairs offering some to the girl, and the girl ignored her. Yes, that sounds plausible. "Maybe she's lost her appetite," Mary finishes, casting a sidelong look at her son.

Connor frowns and looks displeased.

Mary smiles to herself, she's planted the seed.

*

"Do you know what was in that shed?"

When Alia comes in Bronwyn is standing at the sink, washing her hands. She looks up at her mother.

"Sorry?" she asks.

Alia comes up behind her, watching as what looks like blood and mud swirls down the plug hole.

"In the shed," Alia says, her tone short and sharp. "Rifles, machine guns. The police took them all away."

Bronwyn dries her hands on the tea towel and sits down at the table. "It's nothing to do with me."

"But you knew what he was doing, right?" Alia persists. "You knew what he was mixed up in." She stops, plants her hands on the table and shakes her head. "He'll lose his job over this, he'll be inside for God knows how long."

At this Bronwyn looks up. "He lost his job a month ago. They had to let him go."

"Oh, my God," Alia exclaims. "How are you getting on for money? What bills do you owe?" She reaches for her handbag and Bronwyn grabs her hand.

"No, please, it's fine."

"You should come and stay with me, or we'll go away somewhere else." When Bronwyn doesn't reply Alia bangs her hand on the table. "You could be in danger, the British Army are everywhere, looking for people just like him. Like you, by association. Bronwyn, come home to mine, just until it's all sorted out."

Bronwyn barks a short laugh. "It's not going to go away, he's in it for life, you just said that yourself. And it doesn't matter anyway, he won't be coming back here."

Bronwyn sweeps out of the kitchen and Alia hears her thumping up the stairs. She puts her head in her hands and drags her fingers through her hair. What a mess, and it's been a mess for a long time. She hasn't admitted it to herself before, not really, but she's watched for years as Bronwyn has faded away, just existing to do Danny's bidding, and now, though she hates the circumstances, she can't help but grab hold of the tiny bit of hope blooming in her heart that Bronwyn is coming back, taking control.

She gets up and goes to the bottom of the stairs. "I'm going now," she calls. "I'll come back later, okay?"

Alia waits while she puts her coat on. When it is clear she's not going to get an answer she leaves, slamming the door forcefully behind her.

*

Rose is waiting in the lounge when they get back and when she hears the front door open, she stands up, wringing her hands. Connor comes into view, awkward on his crutches. She waits for a beat to see if Mary will appear behind him, and when she doesn't she goes over to him.

"I'm so glad you're home," she says. "How's your leg?"

"It'll mend," he replies and sitting on the couch he pulls her down next to him. "How are you?"

Lonely, scared, worried, she wants to say. Instead she shrugs. "Okay."

"And how are you doing with…," he tails off and she guesses he means his mother.

"This is a nice home," she says, lamely. "You're very lucky."

"But why didn't you have dinner with her last night?" Connor asks. "She just wants to get to know you."

Rose blinks at him. Was she offered dinner last night? She thinks back, doesn't remember Mary mentioning food. As if in answer her stomach rumbles and she covers it with her hand. She actually can't remember the last time she ate anything. She doesn't want to say that to Connor though, she can't tell him that his own mother has offered her nothing because of course she has, a roof over her head and a bed beneath her body.

"We'll eat together tonight, we'll all help in the kitchen."

She is hopeful at his words, now that he's here he can be the buffer between her and Mary. With Connor home, maybe they can finally figure out a way to all live together. She puts her arms around him and buries her face in his neck. He smells like the hospital, of disinfectant and clean bandages.

They are still holding each other when the brick crashes through the front window, landing inches away from their feet. Glass glitters, seems to hang suspended as they pull apart and Rose stares at the shower of shards that follow. Feet thud in the hallway as the front door is opened.

"Bastards!" Rose hears Mary yell.

Connor, pale and silent, struggles to get up as Mary comes into the room. Rose stands, using her hands to push herself up and inadvertently cuts her palms and fingers. As she clenches her fists she feels the tiny pieces of glass cutting into her palms and she winces, holding her hands to her chest as the blood oozes out.

Nobody speaks and Rose looks to Mary, for help, for guidance, for comfort.

Mary is staring at the hole in her window, the net curtain flapping against the cold February air. Finally Mary looks at Rose, then at the shattered glass adorning her living room. She raises her eyes to meet Rose's and Rose blanches.

There will be no living together here, she knows that now. And very slowly she sinks back onto the sofa, sitting amongst the glass, almost primly, and stares down at the glittering carpet.

Chapter 8

February 1981

They've moved me to Long Kesh, and for this I'm relieved. I know a lot of my men are here and even though we may not be in the same cell, I know that they are nearby. It takes my mind off my wife and the constant wondering on why she has not made contact. The only conclusion I can arrive at is that she has been arrested as well. She wasn't anything to do with the attack on her friend's man, even the police will know that, but with relation to the haul they found in my garden shed, well, that, she could have quite easily have been a part of, seeing as it was at our home, which was stupid, I know, but the storage was only supposed to be temporary. Nobody will tell me anything about Bronwyn, she doesn't answer the phone on the scarce times I'm able to make a call, and the duty appointed lawyer (who looks like he just got out of school) gives me a blank look whenever I mention her.

I can ask some people in here though; they will get word to their wives who in turn will find out what the hell is going on. In the meantime, I'm ready for duty. I know what the plans are in the 'H' Blocks, which is where I am headed. Last year my comrades here held a hunger strike which was called off after little more than a month when the British Government appeared to comply with the demands that were set. The requests – that my men are treated as political prisoners as opposed to criminals – were not met. We have five demands for the reinstatement of our Special Category Status; the right not to wear prison uniform or carry out prison work, free association with other prisoners, one letter, one parcel and one visit per week and full restoration of remission lost through the protests. Thatcher fucked with us again, so *we're* going to do it again. It's already started actually, many of the men are already on the blanket and the 'no wash' protest, and I've given my name to volunteer.

As soon as we reach the 'H' Block I'm ordered to strip and change into the prison uniform.

I take a deep breath, face forwards and begin to speak. "I am a prisoner of war. I will not wear a prison issued uniform, nor will I conform to any prison rules."

The screw sighs; he's heard it all before.

He throws me a blanket and leans back against the wall, his arms crossed. I am relieved; I'd heard about the beatings that the guards gave here and I know I'm lucky not to be having the shit kicked out of me right now. So I take my clothes off where I stand and pick up the blanket. I am ordered to walk down to H2 and with my head held high, I don't cover myself with the blanket. Instead, I carry it at my side. I won't show any weakness, of that I am determined.

The H2 wing is comprised of twenty-four cells, a dozen on each side. As I walk down the corridor to my own cell I see my men hanging out of the windowless cell doors, cheering me and banging whatever implements they have to hand. The racket cheers me and takes my mind off the terrible stench.

The odour comes from the men who are already on the 'blanket' and the 'no wash' protest. And it went a lot further than simply not washing. I had been told, we all had, what was happening in the event that any of us on the outside ended up here, inside. They were not slopping out their chamber pots, they were urinating and defecating in them and then flinging them out of the cell bars. They were smearing their excrement on the walls inside using torn pieces of their mattresses as an artist's brush.

As I'm led into my cell I find I am the only occupant and I sit down on the concrete floor. For a moment I feel like I might falter and as my eyes begin to water, maybe from the stench, I bury my face in the scratchy material of the blanket. I've been preparing for this for what seems like all my life, but now it is here it hits me I've not prepared at all. I've read all about the protests and listened as I'm told. But to do it, that's a whole other thing.

As the sound of the screw's footsteps vanishes into the distance, there is a moment of silence. A voice, low, strong and proud, begins to sing. Someone tells the singer to shut up, and then the questions come, thick and fast.

"Who are you, boy?"

"What's your name?"

"Where are you from?"

And then, finally, "Danny Granger, boy, is that you?"

I recognize the voice and I call back. "Sean, is that *you*?"

It was one of my own mates from my I.R.A cell back in Newry. I didn't even know that he was here, let alone why. And it was irrelevant, why we were here. Getting out wasn't important. We had work to do, and for once, that work wasn't on the outside.

No more talking, just action.

*

When the doorbell rings Rose jumps in her seat. It has been an epic failure of a dinner. They cooked it together, as Connor had suggested, but Mary was stony and silent throughout. Rose had tried to ignore the sting on her wounded palms as she washed the potatoes, and Connor kept up an inane chatter throughout the procedure, which only served to annoy Rose and which Mary ignored.

At the sound of a visitor, they all look up.

"I'll go," Mary says, her mouth set in a grim line.

Rose knows she is thinking of the earlier vandals and her heart pounds as she puts down her fork and waits. When she hears Bronwyn's unmistakable voice asking for her she pushes her chair back and runs out into the hall.

"Bronwyn," she says and reaches around Mary to draw her in. "What are you doing here?"

Bronwyn flicks her eyes in Mary's direction. Mary, blocking the door, steps back.

"Dan was arrested," says Bronwyn, dully. "He was the one who shot Connor, him and some others."

"WHAT?" Mary's shout makes Rose jump and before she can act Mary has flung her hand out and grabbed Bronwyn vice-like around her throat.

My God, she's going to strangle her! Rose thinks, but Bronwyn is strong and she bats Mary's hand away. They tussle in silence as Rose watches uselessly. Finally, Bronwyn shoves Mary hard and they stand apart, panting.

And then Connor is there, nudging Rose aside as he stands between his mother and Bronwyn.

"Her man shot you!" Mary shouts, glaring at him now.

"Yeah," Connor answers and looks to Bronwyn.

Rose notices Bronwyn's face flushing a deep red under his stare. "I told on him, I called the police," Bronwyn pauses and looks at all three of them in turn. "I had to tell you, I didn't want you to hear it from anyone else. I'm surprised you hadn't already heard. I'm so sorry."

There is silence now as they all look at her. How would they know? There are no friends who call here to keep Mary in the loop, and nobody speaks to Rose. She looks sharply over at Connor. He didn't seem shocked, had he heard who the gunman was? Did he know at the time? Or has Bronwyn been back to visit him in the hospital without telling her? Rose narrows her eyes, looks back to Bronwyn and tries to take in what she has confessed to doing. You don't call the police on your own husband, not even if the victim is the wife herself, but especially not when it is something that didn't concern her, when it was men's business. Suddenly she is filled with admiration for her best friend, mixed with envy. Bronwyn has always been the bold one, never one to conform to the norm. Danny thought he had knocked that behaviour out of her but it's back.

She's done this for me, thinks Rose. *She's chosen me over her marriage. She cares about me.*

A hidden memory tries to surface, of Bronwyn looking at Connor in the hospital. Rose pushes it away.

She did this for *me*.

Chapter 9

Mary stands and washes up the dinner things while the other three sit at the table and talk quietly. She's not sure how Bronwyn came from scratching at her like an alley cat to being a dinner guest, but she listens intently as Bronwyn talks about how her husband, Danny Granger, is in the I.R.A and how Bronwyn herself pretty much ignored his comings and goings until now. How he's being accused with not only Connor's attempted murder but also a charge of concealing weapons, which the police found in the shed at home. How he was taken to the Newry jail but has now been moved to The Maze.

Mary sneaks a look over her shoulder at the woman. Why now? Yes, she's Rose's best friend and all that, but would anyone risk their marriage or their life for this mouse?

Connor did, her mind whispers. And she can't understand it, not one bit, not at all. The James girl isn't even pretty. She's not smart or motivated or any of the things that would normally turn a man's head.

Her thoughts are more on the husband though, this Danny. Mary realises that she wants to confront him very much. She never had a chance to come face to face with Connor's father's killers. And since then she's stayed well out of it, well away from any trouble and indeed, any people. She has let nobody in for twenty-three years and now the James girl has bought it all to their doorstep and it needs to be stopped. It must be stopped before it goes too far.

She hears a dull crack and she looks down into the washing up bowl. A china cup has cracked in her grip and she lets it go, watches it float around the soap suds.

It's Monday tomorrow. The girl has already stated that she will be going back to work and Connor intends to go to his work, also. Mary has her own plans. Mary is going to sort out a visiting order and take a trip to The Maze.

*

When Bronwyn leaves the Dean house it's very dark. She pulls her coat tighter around her and rubs her hand over her still cramping stomach.

She didn't tell Rose about the miscarriage. She doesn't want anyone to know, not even Danny. It was her baby, her loss.

And she wonders about the irony of it, of this almost-baby coming along now. Why couldn't it have been five years ago, when they were happy together and eager for a family? And when did things change so utterly? She thinks back, back to the excitement of their first home, the plans and the ideas that they shared. They set up camp in the living room while they discussed what to do with the rest of the house. They began work on the kitchen straight away, ripping out all of the old worktops and cupboards. Danny had come home one evening with a van full of pine wood worktops and cupboard doors.

"Where did you get it?" She had breathed as she ran her hand over the varnished wood. "Can we afford it?"

He had winked, told her not to worry about it, said that they were going cheap from a friend of a friend.

They had worked solidly all through the night for a week. They used the skeleton of the old cupboards and affixed the new doors, cut and sanded the worktops until they were exactly the right measurements. Spurred on by Bronwyn's delight at her modern kitchen, Dan had pulled up the lino on the floor and cleaned and scraped and sanded and polished until the natural floorboards looked like something out of a showroom.

One week after the kitchen was finished the 'friend of a friend' found them. His name was Kevin, and the kitchen had belonged to him. He hadn't given it away or even sold it, Danny and his mates had broken into the man's house while he and his wife and family were away and removed every cupboard door and worktop. Her pride and joy was a stolen kitchen.

They had been asleep when Kevin had forced his way into their home, still using the living room as a bedroom, as apart from the kitchen it was the only other habitable space. When the wood splintered on the front door Bronwyn had sat bolt upright, shaking the sleeping Danny's shoulder and whispering urgently in his ear.

Kevin stalked past them, not even giving them a glance as he walked through to the kitchen. He had two heavies with him, one who stood, arms folded, just inside the front door, the other covering the back door. When Kevin evidently saw what he needed to, he returned to the living room and reached for Dan. He battered at him with his fists for such a long time that sweat dripped from Kevin's face. When his arms tired, he uses his heavy boots. All the time Bronwyn screamed, pushing herself back into the corner of the room. She had no fear for herself, but was sure the man wasn't going to stop until Dan was dead.

But stop he did, and as he stood over Danny's bloodied form, he spat down at him. "My men will be back to collect my kitchen tomorrow."

Bronwyn had wanted to take Danny to the hospital, but he refused, so she did her best with salt water and a flannel. His ribs were broken, she was sure of it, and his eyes the next morning were so swollen they were closed. And in the cold light of the next day, she had to watch as piece by piece her new kitchen was dismantled and taken away.

She still had hopes, hopes for her home and her marriage and for the family that would surely come along. Spring had arrived and a new, old fashioned 'make-do' kitchen had been assembled. Bronwyn had started to turn her attention to the garden. She sat outside with a pencil and sketched her ideas for the various sections. Danny didn't want to discuss it, she thought he was still sore from the kitchen debacle and she felt that in his eyes their home had been tainted. So the garden would be her project, a place where she could grow herbs and plant flowerbeds and just sit in the evening sun.

In the first week of April back in 1974 Alia had needed a minor operation, just on her knee with which she had suffered pain since a break years ago had set badly. Bronwyn had elected to stay with her mother upon her release from hospital for a few nights, just to help her out while she grew used to limping around. She remembers the return walk to her own home so well. The sun had come out in force, the evenings were lighter, and as she walked she recited the names of the plants that she had learned and which she was going to grow.

While she had been away the garden had disappeared and it had been transformed into a concrete wilderness.

Now, as she walks up her pathway to the front door she stops and regards her home with a critical eye. She's loathe to leave it, but not sure why. Any happy memories have been quashed by all the bad things that have happened here. Can she start again? Can she do this, live like this, here in this house made for a family, on her own?

She doesn't know, and she doesn't want to think about it tonight.

*

Mary sat and clutched her bag on her lap tightly during the forty minute bus ride to Long Kesh. At some points of the journey, when the bus stops, she almost gets off and returns home. A part of her knows this is utter madness and her actions today are just as likely to bring trouble to her door as that Rose James. But she can't stop herself now, even though this is not the man who killed her lover, he very nearly killed her son. Would she have been making this journey two decades ago if she had the chance, to look the man in the eyes and ask him why? She thinks not, back then she was a tight ball of grief, her only thought was getting through each day and keeping the baby safe and growing inside her.

Today is different; over the last twenty years she has taken that tight ball of grief and used it to harden herself against everything and everyone except Connor.

There are many visitors – more than she expected – making their way into the reception of Long Kesh and she files in beside them, standing tall and firm, making no eye contact. When she reaches the front she hands her bag over to be searched and gives the name of the person she wants to see. Mary expects a reaction, but the guard simply writes Granger's name alongside her own and moves her through to another room.

Her stomach churns noisily and she sips at the water poured from the jugs that have been left on the table for the waiting visitors. She looks at the other people in the room. They mostly look weary, women around her age. Mother's come to visit sons, she supposes. There are a few younger women, some with small children and the kids race around the room shrieking, finding their own play in a room filled with nothing.

A man comes in with a clipboard and reels off a list of names. Hers is among them and she stands up, smooths down her skirt and makes her way towards him. When they are huddled in a group of about half a dozen, he leads them silently out of the door, through a winding corridor. They are deep in The Maze now. The light has been left behind them and for Mary it is like walking into the stinking depths of hell.

They are made to walk alongside cells and she keeps her head straight forward, not wanting to look left or right and see the incarcerated men. Any of them could be the one who killed her man.

The small group is broken off in segments as the guard directs them off towards their loved ones. Finally, it is her turn.

She is shown into a small room, smaller than her little box-room back home, the one that Rose is currently sleeping in. It is simply four walls and it contains two chairs. There is no glass or Perspex divide to separate her and the Granger man. She can't believe this, and she looks back at the guard, sure he has made a mistake using this room. But he has gone, closed the door behind him, shutting her in with this gun-toting lunatic who maimed her boy.

Granger has his back to her and she looks at his thick black hair. He must be cold, for his has a blanket draped over his shoulders. Keeping to the edge of the room she walks around to face him. He looks up at the sound of her footsteps, and a frown creases his features.

"Are you Danny Granger?" she asks.

He nods, doesn't speak, doesn't ask her why she has come.

Though she had practiced in her head what words she was going to use, they are suddenly taken away along with her breath as she sees now that he is clearly naked underneath the blanket. She knows about the protests that are happening here, it's all over the news, but to see it in the flesh, literally, is very strange.

"My name is Mary Dean. My son is Connor Dean."

His mouth works, is he trying to hide a smile? "I know who you are, I got your visiting order."

She stutters, closes her mouth. She must not show her nerves, not to this man. He will use them against her; he will laugh at her, surely, the uncaring, unfeeling bastard that he is.

"And how is our little Rose?" He speaks, finally. "Did she ever come back, or did she carry on running for the hills?"

His mouth is twisted in a spiteful smile and Mary takes a few steps towards him. This is interesting, she had thought he had Rose in mind when he shot Connor, some chivalrous act that however misguided, he thought would be doing the James woman a favour in getting rid of the Protestant. But his tone and his words suggest that he likes Rose as little as Mary does. And if that is the case, why did he do it, if not for her? Maybe they were orders from above, just a lesson to be given to make sure the protestants know the pecking order.

"She came back," she says, cautiously. "But I don't know how long she'll stay."

He clamps his lips together and nods, as though he expected nothing else.

"You know how she came about, right?"

She shakes her head, not really understanding his question and she moves closer still.

"Her mam was raped by one of your lot," he breaks off and laughs, callously. "Fucking ironic, isn't it?"

She sits down in the empty chair, all the fear has gone. "How do you know this?"

He shrugs and with that motion he suddenly looks twenty years younger, like a little boy caught doing something wrong. "I heard Bronwyn's mother talking to one of her mates once. Wasn't supposed to be listening, was I? It's not common knowledge, though I wouldn't be surprised if the whole damn town knows. Rose doesn't though, I don't think."

Oh, he's malicious, thinks Mary. *He's a nasty piece of work.*

"That's my wife, Bronwyn," he goes on. "She's Rose's friend, though God knows why, they couldn't be more different."

"Yes, I've met your wife," replies Mary, absently.

At this Danny springs forward and Mary leans back as far as the chair back will allow her.

"When?" he demands. "When did you see her?"

Mary collects herself, knows she mustn't show him that he scared her. She sits up straight so they are almost nose to nose, "The day after it happened and again just last night, why?"

She suppresses a shiver, clenches her fists to stop her hands fidgeting and wishes she could light up in here. Maybe she can, she looks around, wonders if the guards would even bother to stop her smoking. She knows she has said something wrong, or something that he wasn't expecting. Her mind whirls, trying to make sense of it, going back over her words. It comes to her, a flash in an instant: he doesn't know that Bronwyn was the one who called the police on him. It is a thread of power and one that she intends to use.

Danny breathes heavily and clutches the seat of his chair. He knows the blanket has fallen down around his body. He knows that he is exposing himself to this woman, and he's not comfortable, not like when he's in front of the guards. With them, he couldn't give one shite.

"Was she arrested?" His voice when it comes out is ragged and quiet.

Mary's eyes are bright, "No, why would she have been?"

He can't tell her. He can't say that he thinks she's locked up because if she's not, then why the hell hasn't she been in to see him?

"You don't know, do you?" She whispers the words.

"Know what?" He thinks she's dead or injured, somehow, but she can't be, this Dean woman said she saw her just yesterday. Danny grabs her arm and pulls her towards him. "Know *what*?"

Mary shakes her arm free and looks down at her sleeve, disgusted at his touch. "She was the one who called the police on you. She told them that you shot Connor and all about your stash in your garden shed. She told them everything."

Danny sinks back and stares over Mary's head.

"I want to see my wife," he says.

Mary laughs quietly.

"Listen, listen to me, woman. I want Bronwyn in here. I want you to arrange it."

Mary stops laughing and shakes her head. "I don't even know her; she's just been round at my house while her friend is staying. Once she's gone, which won't be long, believe me, I'll likely never clap eyes on your wife again."

Danny stands up, ignoring Mary as she flinches. He walks around the small room, deep in thought, a plan emerging from a tiny seed that this Mary has planted. He does a few laps, stops behind her and speaks quietly in her ear.

"I can make Rose leave your house. I can get her out of there faster than the bullet went through your son's leg."

At this she does flinch, but recovers well, he notes, as she twists around in her chair and looks up at him. "And in return..?"

Yes, she's quick, this one, Danny thinks with a smile. "You get my wife in here to visit me."

She has a lot of excuses and reasons why it wouldn't work, he can see that in her face, but to her credit she doesn't voice them. Instead, she nods stiffly, stands up and turns to face him.

To him it looks like she doesn't know how to say goodbye. This is no friendship or even a cordial business meeting. There are no words, so she nods, just once, and makes her way to the door.

When the screw comes to collect her and escort her out, Danny takes a deep breath. He picks up the chair that he vacated and raises it over his head. Then he throws it as far as he can. It bounces off the far wall and he flings himself to where it lands, and kicks it repeatedly with his bare feet. When the screws come in they wrap their arms around him, restraining him, one of them landing a thump to his head so hard that he slumps over. They drag him out and he hangs his head, looking down at his toes which are bloodied and raw.

Chapter 10

Mary is exhausted upon her return home to Newry. She hadn't realised how tense she had been throughout the meeting with Connor's shooter, but once she walked through her front door and lay her bag on the kitchen table her body seemed to soften. It was a strange experience, and still wearing her coat she sinks into a chair and lights up a cigarette, pulling on it hungrily.

Now come the worries and the practicalities. She had to get Bronwyn to go to Long Kesh to see her husband. This would be difficult, because Bronwyn didn't seem to be the type of woman to do anything she didn't want to, and if she did want to visit him she would have done so already. And she doesn't want to see him, why would she? If she cared she wouldn't have ratted him out to the police in the first place. And if Bronwyn does go to visit Danny, what if he doesn't like what she has to say to him? Will he still keep his end of the bargain? That bargain, that's another cause for concern. Exactly how does Danny intend to get Rose out of Mary's life? Scare her, most likely, he seems like he is good at scaring people, and whoever he would get on the outside to do it for him would probably be just as thuggish as he is.

Mary is pulled out of her reverie by a tell-tale squeak from an upstairs floorboard. In the silence of the house it sounds very loud, though if she'd had the radio on she wouldn't have even heard it. It must be Connor, and Mary gets up, hurrying up the stairs, worried, for he was supposed to go back to work today. Even though he wouldn't be able to carry out his usual brick-laying work, the manager had agreed to put him on desk duty, helping out with the administration for a while.

"Connor?" She pushes open his door.

The curtains are still drawn, that is the first thing that she notices. Working in the building trade, Connor has always been an early riser, and she tastes dread at the thought of him still being in bed at lunchtime. It must be his leg, maybe he's torn the stitches, maybe it's an infection.

She covers the couple of feet to the bed, touches the shape underneath the cover. "Connor, what's-"

She clamps her mouth shut as a blonde head appears, static charged hair standing on end.

Mary puts her clenched hand to her mouth as she surveys Rose in Connor's bed. Rose stares back at her, eyes wide.

"Get up," Mary says through clenched teeth. "Get out of there."

*

To Rose it looked like Mary was going to say a lot more as she stared down at her in Connor's bed. But she leaves, slamming the bedroom door and Rose sits up, clutches the sheet to her. She peers at the clock and sees it is nearly midday.

She had told the office that she would be back today, though that is the least of her problems. She thinks back, hours ago, when the sound of the door closing had woken her. It was Mary, leaving early, and unable and not wanting to stop herself Rose had crept down the hall to Connor's room. He was awake, sitting on the edge of his bed and he had smiled at her.

"Your mum has gone out," she had said, letting him take her words for how she meant them.

His smile had widened and he had beckoned her over. She had gone, willingly, let him pull her nightie up over her head and toss it aside.

Later, he had left for work, and she had lay back in his bed, knowing she had at least another hour before she had to get up.

But she must have fallen asleep, and now it was lunchtime, and Mary had caught her in Connor's bed. But come on, what the hell did Mary think they did together, play board games or chess?

She had mentioned it to Connor, as she watched him get dressed after they had had sex.

"I don't think your mother likes me," she had said in a small voice.

He had looked over at her then, frowning. "Why? What have you said to her?"

She had paused at that, as the realisation that he would automatically leap to his mother's defence rather than hers. "I don't think I said anything," she had replied. "I'm sure she thinks it's my fault that you got shot, and I can't blame her, it *is* my fault."

He didn't reassure her that she wasn't to blame, she heeded, and her afterglow began to fade.

"You just need to assert yourself, she's a tough woman," he said as he picked up his crutches from where they rested against the wall. "Maybe help out here a little bit, get her onside."

When he had left that was when she closed her eyes. She wasn't overly tired, more that she just didn't want to see anything anymore.

And now the morning had vanished, and Mary was home.

And Mary was angry.

*

Bob, Sue's husband from a few doors down, is fixing the door frame. Bronwyn's mother had arranged it, not happy that even though the door still was able to close and lock in the damaged frame it didn't look very nice. Bronwyn had watched her talking to Sue and later, Bob, and wondered if she should have cared more than she did about the damn door. But he's here now and she's got his money ready, has delved into her sewing cash stash. She offered him a tea, which he gratefully accepted as he fitted a new frame but apart from that she hasn't spoken to him. She can see the new bit of wood from where she sits. Its natural wood, unpainted, and looks out of place with the rest of the white gloss frame. She'll have to paint it. Or maybe strip down white paint from the rest of the door. Whichever she chooses its more work that she really can't find the energy for.

Last night she found two unopened bottles of Liebfraumilch wine, and as soon as Bob leaves she intends to crack open the second bottle. She finished the first last night and she can still taste it now, sour and dry.

Finally he is gone and she goes out to the shed. The police have taken everything except for a couple of tins of paint. She prises the lid off one and looks down at the buttermilk. It's old, it's got a scummy film on top, but it might do for the kitchen. She heaves it up and brings it in, standing it next to the Liebfraumilch bottle. First things first. She pours a generous glass and gulps it down. As she drinks she knows she is sinking down. Her life is becoming a spiral of alcohol infused days. Bitterly she knows that if she still had the baby inside her she would have tipped the Liebfraumilch down the sink. But the baby is gone, buried down by the railway tracks. She knows she should stop thinking about Emma, but it's hard. That is what she's called her, Emma, because she's certain in only the way that a Mother can be that the baby was a little girl. And naming her is one of the worst things she could have done, because ever since she applied that name to her, Emma has become so very real. Too real, such a reality that she has to reach for the wine. And the terrible memory of the Pilsner beers she had that morning, the thought that keeps trying to spring to mind and which she keeps pushing back into a dark corner, did she finish Emma off with the Pilsner?

She sobs, her teeth catching on the edge of the wine glass. And if that is true, if it were the beer, then it's Danny's fault, because she wouldn't have been drinking if he hadn't have been arrested. She can go even further than that, she can blame Rose, for if the stupid girl hadn't got herself involved in a relationship with that Connor, Dan wouldn't have acted and she wouldn't have had to call the police on him.

So it comes full circle and the guilt lies with her oldest friend.

There's a fine rain coming down outside and Bronwyn shudders to think of the sodden grass underneath which Emma rests. She needs more stones or rocks to shelter her little girl. And throwing back the rest of the glass, Bronwyn reaches for her coat. Today she shall go to the forest, the place that she used to go with Dan when they were young and naïve and happy. She'll find the best rocks for her baby, and, she thinks as she puts the half empty bottle of Liebfraumilch at the very back of the cupboard, she will be busy, with no time for any more daytime drinking.

Chapter 11

February 20th 1981

Bobby Sands is starting the hunger strike in nine days' time. Last autumn we were screwed over. Promises were made and broken. This time it will be different. Bobby Sands is going all the way and he has already prepared both himself and us that he will not live to see the final outcome. This time around plans have been carefully drafted. We have all been asked if we would be prepared to volunteer. Dozens of men put their names forward and it has been decided that these strikes will be staggered for maximum publicity. I have given my name, there is no question, no soul searching, this is me and it's what I'll do. I'm in a better position that some of the men, I have no family apart from Bronwyn. My parents never really existed, not to me anyway, and I have no siblings. There are no children of mine to lend a second thought. There is no question.

I don't expect it will go all the way. I have a good chance of coming out of this. I'm not starting first, that's down to Bobby. I think I'm about fifth in line and due to commence my hunger strike in around the second week of March. Also, Thatcher will concede to our five demands. She has to, she can't be seen to allow people to die, even if her own iron will won't let her see it, her advisors will.

Right now I'm still on the blanket and 'no-wash' protest. The hunger strike will be nothing like this, nothing can be as bad as this. I mean, it will be difficult not eating, but not impossible. I've been hungry before, many times.

Today I awoke after a fitful sleep. I never thought any place could be colder than the Kidds Road house, but my cell is. At least at home I can put on extra clothing or get another blanket. And no matter what faults I found with the house, I know I'd never wake up with maggots stuck to me like I did this morning.

I pulled them off my skin, retching. The flies get in, attracted by our shite that covers the walls and so after, later, come the maggots.

I wonder if Bronwyn will come in today, if that mad Mary has made her see sense. The Dean woman might not even have seen her yet to convince her. I need to be patient. I know that, and I can be. I'm not going anywhere.

I think some more about Mary Dean. I'll admit that she intrigued me. Parents always do, probably because I never had any of my own. And yet they are all so different. Look at Bronwyn's mother and Mary. Alia has always seemed too eager to please, letting Bronwyn get away with murder, as if she was afraid her daughter would walk out and never return. And yet Mary, she seems to be a proper mother, looking out for her boy. I wonder why she came to see me, sitting there looking at me like I was some sort of exhibit in a zoo. I barely remember shooting her son; I was sent out to do a job and I done it. We have to keep at it, showing that we are in control, telling them through our actions what we want. Christ, it's not like we killed him or anything and to be honest, from what I've heard, the shot was off anyway, it barely grazed his skin. I don't like to dwell on that too much, I've never been a poor shot, I don't know what happened that night. I think of Mary and how she doesn't like Rose. That's interesting, I could think of worse women that her precious son could end up with. The one thing about Rose is that she is compliant, willing to please. She'll never cheat on him, she'll be a good daughter in law and she'll have his dinner waiting on the table every evening without fail. Sometimes though, compliance isn't enough. Sometimes you want someone to shout back at you. You want a spark, a firecracker, like my Bronwyn. Keeps it interesting, doesn't it?

I wonder if Mary Dean will come again. If she does it means she wants me to get rid of Rose. I can do that, being inside won't stop me. That wouldn't be hard at all.

This life right now, with the cold and the maggots, that is hard.

But it can only get easier.

Everything can only get easier.

*

Mary stiffens as she hears Rose up and about upstairs. She closes her eyes, and snaps them open quickly when all she sees behind her eyelids is the girl in her son's bed. Oh, she's not so old and out of touch that she is naïve to what happens between the youth of today, but she also knows the part of their body that men think with, and how a woman uses her flesh to get what she wants. She's got to be careful, Mary reminds herself. She needs to push Rose away but not Connor with her.

Finally, the sound of Rose plodding down the stairs comes to Mary's ears, and she prepares herself. The girl comes around the corner, hesitating on the threshold of the kitchen.

"Breakfast?" Mary's voice is far from friendly, but just the offer seems to throw Rose off balance.

"Yeah, please," Rose replies, guardedly.

The girl is wary, but willing as she comes in and sits down in the empty chair facing Mary. She perches on the edge of the seat, as if ready to take flight at any moment. Mary is silent as she boils the kettle and busies herself getting fresh tea cups and plates out of the cupboard.

"I didn't realise that you were not a full Catholic," Mary says her carefully thought out and prepared words as she pours the water into the teapot. "You've got a little bit of us in you. Who would have thought?"

As she carries the pot and cups to the table she chances a look at Rose's face. As she expected, the girl looks confused.

"Excuse me?"

"Well, I know it's not the same thing, obviously," Mary trills a little laugh that sounds so very false to her own ears. She cringes, but pushes on, taking a deep breath. "It must have been difficult, the circumstances. Do you ever see your father?"

Rose shakes her head and looks dazed. "My mother doesn't speak about him." She lowers her eyes and says, almost shyly, "I don't know who he is."

Mary feigns surprise, wills her face to redden as if she has been caught out. She begins to speak, tripping over her words purposefully. The girl is so *slow* though, just gawping at her. "I'm sorry," Mary demurs. "I shouldn't have said anything."

It actually takes long minutes of silence, which Mary uses to fill a milk jug, before Rose appears to find the words.

"Hold on, do you know my father?"

A little bit of tea has dribbled from the teapot spout, and Mary goes over to the sink to retrieve a new dishcloth from the cupboard.

"Just that he was a Protestant," she says, casually, her back towards Rose. "Just that he raped your poor mother."

There's a beat of yet more silence. Not a sound from behind her as Mary makes a show of rooting through the cupboard for the cloth, even though she can clearly see a new packet right in front of her. She can hear the girl breathing heavily behind her. Strange snuffling noises grow louder, like the sound that a newborn baby makes before breaking into a cry.

"Ah, I knew I had some," she says, standing upright and holding up the pack triumphantly.

But when she turns around Rose has vanished, her tea left untouched, and Mary is alone in the kitchen.

*

Bronwyn, as always, is Rose's first port of call. She hammers on the front door, and when there is no answer she opens the side gate and goes into the back garden, peering through the kitchen window. There is no sign of life, and Rose leaves, closing the gate softly behind her.

She walks on, not back to Connor's, but towards her own home, scuffing the soles of her boots along and trying not to think of Mary's words. Could they be true? Or did Mary really dislike her that much, that she would speak so cruelly?

Soon she is at her own front door, letting herself in, recoiling again from the aroma in the hallway. She doesn't look for her mother, instead she heads for the kitchen and the old tin where Kathleen keeps all her papers and documents. It is where it always is, at the back of the pantry. She pulls it down, opens it up and tips the contents onto the kitchen table. She roots through home insurance certificates and receipts and finds at the very bottom of the pile her birth certificate. Snatching it up she scans it, noting that the father's name is blank. She doesn't know what she expected, and a blank space doesn't mean anything, does it? She pushes the tin to one side and covers her face with her hands. She is shaking and she wraps her hands around herself. The tremors running through her body are not due to the cold though, they are a result of Mary's wicked words. Why would she say what she did? It's beyond spiteful, it's cold-blooded and evil. Just vicious.

"What are you doing?"

Her mother's voice makes her jump, and she spins around to face her.

Kathleen lurches over to the other side of the kitchen, all the while looking at Rose out of dull, dead eyes. As she moves, Rose smells the alcohol along with an unwashed, stale smell and clothes that give off the scent of fried food.

"Connor's mother says that you were raped, and that's where I come from," Rose blurts out the words before she can change her mind.

She wants to add on a plea, *tell me it isn't true*, but she forces herself to stay quiet.

"Connor's mother," repeats Kathleen, as she stumbles and leans against the worktop to support herself. "Connor's mother says that, does she?"

Rose nods. "It's a lie though, isn't it, why would she say something so cruel?"

Kathleen shrugs and turns away, but not before Rose sees the tears shining in her mother's eyes. The emotion is something that Rose isn't used to seeing, not that sort anyway. Anger and a cold demeanour are usual, tears are not. She takes the little piece of sentimentality and moves across the room towards Kathleen. Kathleen, seeing her approach, reaches blindly for the handle on the back door.

"Don't touch me!" she shrieks, and pulling open the door she blunders into the back garden.

"Mam, please stop," Rose calls as she follows her mother down the very bottom of the garden.

They reach the fence and Kathleen turns, wildly seeking a way out.

"Just... go, won't you?" Kathleen wipes her sleeve across her face, a trail of tears and mucus clinging to her top. "You should have stayed away, you shouldn't come back here." Kathleen pauses, seems to catch her words and then lets them tumble free anyway. "I don't want you here!"

Rose flinches as though she was physically punched. She wants nothing more than to leave, but she's come this far, she's questioned her mother about something that she must find the answer to. Because she thought that Mary was being hateful with her painful words, but her own mother's reaction has planted doubt in Rose's mind. Suddenly it's the most important thing in the world, that when she leaves this house for the last time, it is with the facts, though even as she thinks this she wonders if she really should know the truth. Sometimes, lies are easier both to tell and to live with. She makes to speak again, to ask it once more, but Mary holds up her hand.

"Yeah… yes. Yes." Mary speaks the same word, several times, choking on sobs.

She is underwater, a strange sensation running throughout her whole body and guilt is the one that burns the fiercest. *I'm going to faint*, thinks Rose. *I'm going to fall down right here on the garden path*. So sure that she is on the verge of collapse, Rose goes quickly down onto her knees. She focuses on the weeds growing between the paving slabs and feels the hard concrete underneath her hands. She can hear her mother, breathing heavily and still choking on her tears. *Oh, my poor mam, how much she must hate me…* The lightheaded feeling passes, but still Rose doesn't get up. She rubs the pads of her fingers up and down the path, the rough ground catching on her fingers. It seems a long time later when she catches the rancid scent of Kathleen as she moves past her and she chances a look up and behind her. Her mother has gone back into the house, and the door is closed behind her. After a moment, Rose hears the scrape of the inside bolt pulled across.

She remains in a kneeling position, blinded by unshed tears, and she leans forward and vomits onto the grass.

Chapter 12

The forest is deathly quiet, Bronwyn had only passed a couple of dog walkers braving the cold on her own journey there, and she relishes the alone time. She had taken a bus to Chapel Road and then walked the rest of the way. She picks up the trail that she used to walk with Danny and after walking for about fifteen minutes she stops. She doesn't want Danny to be a part of this expedition; this is solely for her and Emma. Bronwyn changes direction, walking off the track and into the forest. There is no footpath here but she enjoys the crunch of the dead leaves beneath her feet. It's wet in parts; the rain has seemed relentless since last autumn. She catches sight of a fallen branch and remembers the last time she came here, back in the wood collecting days.

They had found an axe, just a small, hand-held one, in the shed when they moved into the Kidds Road house. Danny had been overjoyed at his find, brandishing it around and playing the fool, making Bronwyn laugh with his antics. They had bought it here to the forest and he had hacked away at small branches of younger trees. It wasn't very sharp, it was practically blunt, and before their next visit Danny had cleaned it with steel wool and sharpened the blade with a flint and a file. The next time they were in the forest she had sat back while he hacked away and they had returned home with enough firewood to get them through the winter. She can't recall which winter that was, maybe seven or eight years ago now.

She kicks at a pile of leaves absentmindedly. Maybe she'll put the electric fire upstairs in her bedroom and get the real wood fire going again. Maybe eventually she'll find someone else to sit in front of the flames with.

She shakes her head, it's not time for that sort of thinking. For a long while it's just going to be her, her and Emma and the thought of what might have been.

Soon she comes across the duck pond and she carefully sets her bag down at the edge. She crouches down at the edge of the bank and plucks some pebbles from the icy cold water. They are good ones, worn smooth from years of being in the free flowing stream, making a century old journey and eventually ending up here in this pond. She puts them in the carrier bag that she bought for this purpose, and then moves up into the meadow. Heather is growing in abundance here, suited to the acidic soil. She pulls a few pieces up and wetting the roots, in the bag they go. Heather will look nice in the garden, especially down by the railway track.

As she heads out of the forest and back towards the bus stop, she feels lighter and this time when the hope springs she lets it in. No more dulling it with drink, she tells herself sternly.

As she walks down the main road, swinging her bag of stones and heather, she wonders about getting a lump hammer and maybe smashing the concrete up from the Kidds Road garden.

She passes a group of three British soldiers. They stand casually in someone's front garden, following her down the road with their eyes.

"Supergrass!" One of them with shorn dark hair and bright blue eyes shouts across the road to her.

Bronwyn looks over at them, wondering if she heard correctly. His mates take up the chant, the melody rising into a crescendo. It sounds like a football chant. "Super, supergrass, grassy-grasshopper, SUPERGRASS!"

The term is well known and they are calling her an informer, adding the grasshopper, which means 'copper' in rhyming slang, line in for their own amusement. So everyone, even the Brits know, that she had her own husband arrested. The implications of this being common knowledge doesn't escape her and clutching the bag tightly she turns away from the soldiers, tucks her chin in and walks quickly on, head down.

*

"I think I done something really stupid."

Mary pounces on Connor as soon as he limps through the front door, taking his arm and guiding him through to the living room.

He leans against the couch and tilts his head on the side as he regards his mother.

"Why, what did you do?"

She closes the door to the living room and lowers her voice, even though Rose isn't here. Mary wrings her hands, pastes what she hopes is a worried expression on her face.

"I didn't realise that Rose didn't know about her father." She stops talking and slaps at Connor's arm. "You should have told me!"

"What? What?" Connor leans forward. "I don't know what you're talking about."

"Oh, God," Mary whispers and covers her mouth with her hands. "*You* don't even know?"

"No!" He exclaims. "Where is she? What's happened?"

Mary sinks down onto the sofa and groans. "I didn't realise that she didn't know that her mother was raped, and Rose was the product of it." She looks up through her lashes at her son, somewhat pleased with the expression of disbelief that he wore. "I don't think she knew, and she went off somewhere, I've not seen her since."

Connor deflates before her very eyes. Mary watches him carefully. Is it a look of disgust on his face now? Knowing that he's let *that* into his life and his bed and his heart? He snaps his head up and glares at his mother.

"How do *you* know?"

She has prepared for this question. In fact, she was surprised that Rose didn't ask it herself earlier.

"I went to town, early this morning. You know what the women are like around here, they must have heard that she's here, they couldn't wait to tell me." She sighs, deeply. "I presumed it was common knowledge, I mean if *they* all knew, surely she did?"

"She never mentioned anything to me," says Connor as he struggles to maintain an upright position. "I'll have to see if I can find her."

Mary nods, eagerly. "Please tell her I'm so very sorry, I just didn't know…,"

He looks at her long and hard as he leaves the house, the door banging harder than normal behind him. Mary gets up and goes into the kitchen. Was it too much, her last words? Mary doesn't apologise to anyone, even if she's in the wrong. Did Connor pick up on that? Did he see through her?

She shakes her head to dispel the thought and flicks on the oven. As she moves around the kitchen she gets out the things for dinner. Connor will be hungry when he returns, with or without the girl. She gets two plates out and puts them under the grill to warm. Even if she comes back with Connor, Rose won't want any dinner, of that Mary's sure.

*

Bronwyn hears someone knocking on her door, but she's down by the railway track and she doesn't want to leave yet. It might not even be her door, she reasons, perhaps one of the neighbours has visitors. Or it might be people from her own community, come to batter her for grassing up Danny. She ignores it but soon though, she hears the gate open and close and round the side of the house Connor comes into view. She thinks of staying low, let him think that nobody is home, but, almost against her will, she raises her hand.

"I'm down here," she calls.

She shouldn't draw attention to herself, not with the new 'supergrass' tag. Connor's presence in her own home could tip those who disagree with her actions over the edge, but he is here now, picking his way towards her.

He remains standing when he reaches her, looking around, over to the bridge and then the field beyond.

"What are you doing here?" He asks, finally, squinting down at her.

Surely I should be asking that, she thinks to herself. She looks down at the mound of stones she has made from those she collected earlier in the forest.

"It's Emma," she says, as she picks up two large stones. They are almost onyx black, shiny and with silver grey stripes encircling the width of them. They are her favourite in her collection, these ones. She glances up at him. "Emma's the baby I lost." She says by way of explanation.

"I'm sorry," he says and to her surprise he goes down into an awkward crouch next to her. "Was this recent?"

She nods. So recent, so raw, and yet it seems like Emma has always been known to her. She looks away from him, the sympathy in his eyes isn't what she wants so she changes the subject.

"What are you doing here, anyway?"

"Looking for Rose," he replies. "Have you seen her?"

Bronwyn shakes her head. "Not lately."

"Shit," he swears, softly.

All isn't right in the world of the happy couple, she thinks. She lets out an involuntary shudder and it dawns on her they are sitting on the damp grass and the day is losing the light.

"Do you want a drink?" she asks.

"Yeah. That would be good."

He pushes at the ground, trying to straighten his bad leg and she grips his upper arm, hauls him upright.

"It's not easy, is it?" she comments, looking at his injury.

"No," he replies as they walk slowly back towards the house. "It's not easy at all."

But as she holds the door open for him, she gets the impression he is not talking about his gunshot wound.

"How are things at home?" she asks.

"Not good, really," he starts and then clams up. "Sorry, I shouldn't have come here. You've got enough on your plate."

"Do you know what? I've really not. I've got nothing going on at all, I've no husband, no baby. No friends since word spread of me grassing on Danny. I could actually do with hearing about someone else's problems." She laughs as she says the words, but as soon as they are out of her mouth she reflects on how shallow they sound.

His smile tells her he didn't take offence, and he points at the jar of coffee she gets off the shelf. "Got anything stronger than that?"

She remembers the Liebfraumilch and retrieves it from the back of the cupboard. It's very tempting to join him in finishing off the bottle, but she's had a good day and she doesn't want it to finish badly. Besides, she's chilled to the bone from spending almost all day outside, and a coffee will help warm her.

"Where is she, then?"

Connor shrugs. "I don't know, she took off earlier today and we've not seen her since. Listen, do you know anything about her father?"

Bronwyn shifts, uncomfortable about discussing her friend's private business. Her thoughts of earlier come back to her, and she pinches her lips together. It's partially Rose's fault that Bronwyn is now alone, and more than a bit her fault that this man in front of her is limping along with a bullet wound.

"What do you know?" she asks, cautiously. As much as her feelings about Rose are leaving a bitter taste at the moment, she still doesn't want to throw her under the bus.

"That her mother was raped and gave birth to Rose."

Bronwyn passes him a glass and the bottle of wine, "sounds about right."

"But Rose never knew? How did you know, if she didn't know?"

"I think my mother found out, I heard her discussing it once with one of the women who had heard the rumour." She scoops some coffee granules into her mug and then pauses, spoon suspended. "Wait, has Rose found out?"

Connor grimaces. "It seems that way. It looks to me like it was common knowledge to everyone except the person who it actually involved."

Oh God, he sounds judgemental now and she swings around to face him, suddenly furious. "I never told anyone because it was none of my business!"

He holds his hands up in a gesture of surrender. "I didn't mean it that way, of course it wasn't down to you to tell her."

Her anger dissipates and as the kettle boils she fills the mug to the brim and brings it over to the table where she sits down heavily.

"No good would ever come of her knowing the truth about her parents. Rose shouldn't have ever found out, she's too fragile for something like that."

"Not like you."

She tilts her head as she regards him, wondering whether it is a joke or a compliment.

"Rose and I grew up differently. I always looked out for her."

He pushes the wine away, barely touched, and stands up. "I need to keep looking for her."

She walks to the door, holds it open for him.

"Will you come along tomorrow and see her, I think she could do with a friend?" he asks as he balances on the step and positions his crutches.

"Yeah, maybe," she remembers the soldiers chanting at her earlier and can't see herself wanting to leave the house much at all in the future.

She has almost pushed the door closed when she catches his voice, thrown back over his shoulder as he shuffles down to the gate. "I'm sorry about Emma, Bronwyn," he calls.

Even though he has his back to her she shuts the door quickly, not wanting him to see the sudden tears in her eyes. She hurries back to the kitchen and sits down in the seat that he vacated. Her baby's name, her *own* name, on his lips.

Without thinking she picks up the wine that he left and gulps it down until the glass is empty.

*

Rose spends the rest of the day in the park. She can't recall walking there, she can't even remember getting up off her knees in her mother's garden. She looks behind her at Gallows Hill and the fact she is on the former hanging site barely registers. Usually she avoids walking here, let alone sitting all day.

The light has faded now, but she literally has nowhere else to be. Bronwyn might be home by now, but she doesn't think her legs will carry her over to Kidds Road. Her energy has gone. Everything inside her seems to have gone.

She looks across towards Church Street. In the gloom she can just about make out the spire of Saint Patrick's and the outline of the surrounding stone walls. It's an Anglican place of worship, and she wonders if Mary has ever gone there to seek solace. As she thinks of Mary she ponders about what prompted her to question Rose's parentage. And who had told her? Going purely on Kathleen's own reaction it was certainly the truth, but who else knew? And how did Mary find out? She can't have friends from Rose's side of the tracks, that's for sure.

As she sits in the half light and thinks about it, she notices a figure walking up the hill towards her. Rose stiffens as the person seems to be heading directly for her. She lets out her breath, sees it in a fog in front of her, and she realises it is Mary, but she's not sure if she is fearful or relieved. She waits until Mary reaches her and looks down upon her.

"You'll catch your death out here," Mary comments, quietly. "Shall we get you home?"

Her words are kind, unexpected, and the mention of the word 'home' cracks Rose open all over again. She can hardly feel the tears on her frozen face, but she knows that she is crying by the sobs that catch in her throat. She pushes herself upright and stands still, waiting for her body to catch up with her head. Mary has turned and is headed back the way she came. Rose forces her feet to follow her.

Once they are back at Mary's house, Rose stands in the doorway of the kitchen. She feels useless, cold, and her body is shaking, tremors that once again she can't control. The oven is on and she looks towards it, wonders if it would be dreadfully impolite to go and sit next to it for a bit, just while she thaws out a little.

"I've got some stew saved, if you're hungry?" Mary says as she unwinds her scarf from around her neck and loops it over the back door handle.

She can't imagine that she'll ever eat anything again, but as Mary pulls on her oven gloves and takes the casserole dish out the aroma lingers in the air. The stale smell of Rose's old house that had assaulted her nostrils all day is buried momentarily under the lamb and rosemary fragrance.

"Oh, yes, please." Rose's voice is hoarse and scratchy, still clogged with tears, but all of a sudden she finds that her feet will move and she sits down in the chair nearest the oven as Mary ladles the dinner out onto a pre-warmed plate.

As she sits at the table she follows Mary around the kitchen with her eyes. The older woman is humming a tune which sounds like *The Tide is High*, by Blondie. It's strange to hear something happy and light hearted coming out of the stern Mary's mouth, but it is nice. Suddenly this kitchen is like Bronwyn's home used to be, back when they were children, with Alia turning up the radio and bopping around the room to The Supremes or The Rolling Stones as she made them hot chocolate with whipped cream and marshmallows.

Rose relaxes and picks up her fork, suddenly ravenous.

*

Mary busies herself in the kitchen, but all the time she watches Rose as she at first picks at the lamb stew, and then crams it down her throat. She doesn't even cut up the meat, which Mary cooked in large chunks to maintain the flavour and juices. She's eating like a pig, but Mary forces herself not to comment and instead runs a glass under the tap and passes the water to Rose.

She wonders when the girl will think to ask about Connor's absence, and then as though she had sent a subliminal message, Rose looks up.

"Where is Connor?"

Mary hesitates, sweeping some errant crumbs from the table into her hand and brushing them into the bin. She glances at the clock.

"Probably he's gone for a drink with some of the men from work," she says, and notes Rose's crestfallen expression with satisfaction.

"Does he know, about what you told me earlier?"

"Your father, you mean?" Mary hides a smile as Rose winces noticeably. "I'm not sure, to be honest I presumed everyone knew."

The girl's face turns deathly pale at this and she puts her fork gently on the side of her plate. At the same time, Mary's keen ears hear the tell-tale click of Connor's crutches outside the front door. Mary moves quickly into the hallway, pulling the kitchen door closed behind her, and she's waiting as Connor unlocks the front door and hobbles in.

"The girl is here," she says to him in a low voice. "She feels very bad about everything, best not to mention that you've been out looking for her."

Connor looks tired, she notes, and a flame of anger flares up in her chest. He can barely walk, he shouldn't have been traipsing all over Newry looking for the selfish girl.

"All right," he says, and lowers himself onto the bottom stair to prise his boots off. "If you think it's best."

"I do, I've been chatting to her, she's eating dinner right now. Just tell her you let your workmates take you out for a beer, or something."

With the instructions that will cover her issued, she pats him on the shoulder and retreats back into the kitchen.

Rose is standing at the sink, rinsing the plate that contained the stew which she must have scraped into the bin. As Mary comes back in the room she turns, sees Connor in the hall, and she wipes her hands on the towel and pushes past Mary to go and greet him.

Mary moves over to the sink, looks at the plate which still has traces of gravy on it. Sighing, she turns on the hot tap and gets the washing up liquid out from underneath the sink.

*

She can still taste the Liebfraumilch in her mouth when she wakes up the morning after Connor's visit. She turns over and faces the wall, remembering now not only finishing Connor's glass, but the whole bottle. There is no more alcohol left in the house now, so today could be the start of a new beginning. She thinks of the half-hearted plans and ideas she has thought up over the last few days; the painting of the kitchen and taking a sledge hammer to the concrete outside. Thought processes that when put into action will make her start to live again, to do something for her own happiness and contentment. Something that will take Emma's place.

Emma.

Bronwyn sighs and flips onto her back. As soon as the shops open she'll go down, pick up some supplies with her sewing money. Maybe a nice piece of meat from the butcher, and some fresh vegetables. She needs to start eating better. She needs to build up her strength.

She makes a mental shopping list, adding treats that she wouldn't usually splash out on. She won't get wine.

She promises herself, she won't buy any wine.

*

They had a special on Guinness, down at Murphy's on Monaghan Street. When she had seen it in the window, the fluorescent stickers showing the sale price, she had remembered she had promised Connor she would go and see Rose later, and she reasoned that she could take a few tins with her. Who knows, it might even loosen Mary up a little.

She takes the food out of the carrier bags and inspects her wares as she puts them away. Most of this will be thrown away; it's hard to buy groceries for one. She had conceded and bought a whole chicken. She intends to cook it one night when Alia is visiting and then she can have it cold the day after. She wonders what night her mother would like to come to dinner and worries that she won't be able to stand it. The pretence, on Bronwyn's part, that everything is fine and the worry that will be evident on her mother's face, even as she tries not to say the wrong thing.

It's too much to think about, her head is full and she slams her hand down on the counter. When did everything become so difficult? When did even just thinking and planning become too much, too hard?

She abandons the shopping and reaches for a can of beer.

*

She's drunk as she takes a slow walk to Connor's house. She's aware of that, and she takes deep breaths of the cold air and tests herself by walking in a straight line. The cans of Guinness clink against each other in her bag and she puts her hand in her jeans pocket, rubbing her fingers over one of the onyx-like stones she slipped in there after she'd been sitting with Emma earlier in the day.

It's a good hour walk, and she could have taken the bus, but her body feels sluggish and she wants to wake it up. She remembers how in her younger days she ran this route. She was a good runner. Her school put her in for all of the county competitions, cross country, track, even hurdles at one time. There was a memorable run back in 1969, the year before she had married Danny. They had moved into the Kidds Road house and she was still training every day. There was rioting that had begun in Derry and protests had started up all over Northern Ireland. Danny had not been home for two days, he never told her but she imagined she knew where he was, in Belfast or Crossmaglen, right in the thick of it. Alia begged her to stay inside, but Bronwyn refused to be told what to do in her own town. She had left the house early, starting with a gentle jog across the fields. It was hot already, it was going to be another scorcher, and after five miles she decided to turn around and head back.

She was running through Hill Street, noticing how eerily deserted the usually busy road was. Up ahead she could see an armoured vehicle and she slowed, knowing there would be soldiers with it. And with the soldiers came the people who fought them, those like Danny. There were no side roads to divert her route, so she made the decision to keep going. Keeping close to the brick walls of the shop fronts she put her head down and broke into a sprint. They came flooding out of the warehouse gates as she passed; balaclava wearing, gun toting fighters. They shoved her out of the way and she raised her arms to protect her head. One of them seemed to reach out for her and she elbowed him as she passed. From the other side the soldiers appeared, rushing the fighters. Water cannons started from somewhere in the street, aiming in her direction. Something whizzed past her face and exploded over the road, causing thick smoke and hot flames, and rubber bullets thudded into brickwork. The gunfire started and she ran on, low to the ground, seeing the end of the group of I.R.A men. As she passed the end she heard the thump of a bullet as it connected with skin. Something wet hit her face but she ignored it and sprinted on.

Two miles later she thundered through her front gate and collapsed on the porch step. It wasn't unusual for her to shake after a hard run, but this was something more. Her hands wouldn't work, stuck in claw-like positions, tense and stiff. With great difficulty she had taken the key from under the gnome that stood on the step and after several attempts at reaching up and inserting it into the lock she had given up, dropped the key, and lay in a foetal position at her front door.

She had lain there for hours, blood-stained and dehydrated. She didn't remember finally getting into the house or taking a bath, though she knows she must have done on her own eventually. Alia didn't call round and Danny stayed away another three days.

She never told Dan about that day nor anyone else. But it was the last day she had ever gone running.

*

Now, on that same route, she thinks about running again. It has been twelve years, her body, though still slim, is soft and squashy. She remembers how it used to feel, the running, and how her hair and skin used to glow with health and vitality.

As she considers it there's a part of her telling her that yet again she's making another plan, a half-hearted one, which is all good in theory but why doesn't she just do it instead of always contemplating?

Maybe I will, she thinks, determined as she picks up her pace and carries on towards Connor's house.

Inside her bag the cans continue to clink together, mocking her almost as she tries to move on.

*

Rose conceals herself in Connor's bedroom. She's not in his bed, so it's okay to be here, she figures. Connor's not in here either, he's outside the front of the house, sitting on the step, waiting for God knows what.

He hasn't mentioned anything about her father and she thinks maybe Mary didn't tell him. Although someone will, if somebody told Mary then it seems likely he will hear about it, eventually. Idly she wonders what her mother is doing today. How does she feel now that the truth is out? Is she relieved, finally happy that she can stop pretending to love her daughter and not have to see her again? Rose thinks it is more likely Kathleen will never be happy again. She should have aborted Rose, gone to a back street doctor or made the crossing to England while she had the chance, thirty years ago she could have got rid of the problem and started over with a husband and gone on to have proper children. It explains the lack of family on Kathleen's part, anyway. Her grandparent's would have kicked Kathleen out, moved her cross country and disowned her.

Rose shakes her head and looks out of the window again. Connor is standing now, slowly approaching the gate. Rose feels an itch on her forearm and scratches at it, absentmindedly. Where is Connor going now? And why is he outside in just a thin jumper on such a cold day?

She sees his arm raised in greeting and she follows the direction in which he is looking in, sees her friend, Bronwyn, walking quickly down the street.

There is a letter opener on Connor's window sill and Rose picks it up, scraping now at the itch on her arm. Why is Bronwyn here? Mary won't be pleased, Rose's sure of that. Still she doesn't move, instead she narrows her eyes and continues watching, unnoticed behind the net curtain.

Bronwyn reaches the gate and Connor opens it. They are talking; Bronwyn holds up her bag and Connor nods, says something that causes Bronwyn to break out into a laugh. Rose scratches with the letter opener, harder now. It's been ages since she's seen Bronwyn laughing.

Rose shifts position at the window, moving a couple of feet to get a better view. The two of them are serious now, their heads bent close together. Bronwyn's eyes are downcast as she talks. Rose's breath catches in her throat as Connor's hand comes up and he strokes at Bronwyn's arm. Then its round her shoulders in what seems to be a protective embrace, and slowly the pair make their way up to the house.

Rose hears the front door close behind them.

She puts the letter opener back where she found it. She doesn't notice that the pointed end is covered in blood.

Pulling down her sleeves and straightening her skirt, Rose knows she should go downstairs to meet her friend. Instead, she sits down on the end of the bed, and waits.

*

"Connor said you might come round," said Mary as Bronwyn came through to the kitchen, followed by Connor. "I've not got much in but there's some tea if you're hungry."

"Oh, cheers." Bronwyn casts a look at Connor and he smiles in return.

Mary watches as they both take a seat at the table. The dinner is what she would call a 'make-do' meal using whatever is in the cupboards, but it's not a bad one. There is ham, salad, some celery in a pint glass and new potatoes covered in butter.

"I always think salads are a summer food," says Mary as she carries three plates to the table. "But I've got an apple pie in the oven. We can warm ourselves with that after."

Out of the corner of her eye Mary sees a shadow at the bottom of the stairs and knows its Rose. The girl makes no move to come into the room, however, and as Mary moves around the table to get the cutlery out of the drawer, she closes the door that leads to the hall.

"Um, is Rose not joining us?" Bronwyn asks, her back to the door, as she helps herself to a ladle full of potatoes.

Mary shrugs and looks at Connor.

"I'll go and get her," he offers.

"No, you rest that leg of yours," says Mary. "I'll go."

Mary opens the door and slips out, noting that the shadow of Rose is no longer in the hallway. She walks upstairs, slowly and deliberately. The door to both Connor's room and the spare room in which Rose sleeps are closed. Mary waits for a minute. She can hear nothing behind either door.

She goes back downstairs and into the kitchen, gives Connor and Bronwyn a look of helplessness.

Nothing is said. Connor looks downcast, Bronwyn shakes her head. Mary turns away and smiles to herself.

The meal is a bit of a stilted affair and they eat in silence. After the plates are cleared away, (by Bronwyn, Mary notes with approval), the pie is bought out of the oven.

"Would anyone care for a beer?" Bronwyn picks up her handbag and pulls out a pack.

Mary has never been much of a drinker and she swallows her distaste at the sight of the young woman holding the pack of Guinness aloft. On the other hand, alcohol seems ideal for what she is about to try and talk her guest into doing. "Why not?" says Mary.

She collects glasses, semi-aware that they would generally just drink from the can. But she has them now, and obediently they fill the half pint glasses.

Mary waits until Bronwyn has finished her first. She tops it up and looks over to Connor.

"Go and try to get Rose down here," she instructs. "Her friend has come across town to see her, after all."

Connor obliges, forgoing his crutches and limping out of the room.

"I wanted to speak to you alone," says Mary as she refills her own wine glass. "Have you been to see your husband?"

Bronwyn looks surprised. "No," she replies. "I don't think it's a good idea."

Mary takes a deep breath, knowing that Connor could be back any minute, she needs to be quick. "I'm not a Catholic, but it doesn't mean I don't keep up to date with what is going on in the world. There are many men, like your husband, in that prison and I heard that almost all of them have volunteered for the next hunger strikes."

"You think Danny would be involved?" Bronwyn laughs. "He wouldn't... he's not into anything like that, he prefers the action. Hunger strikes are too political for him."

The genuine sympathy that she feels surprises Mary. She suppresses it, thinks instead inwardly how foolish and naive Bronwyn is. Outwardly, she smiles and lays a hand on top of Bronwyn's.

"What do you think the attack on Connor was about? It's all politics, it's not personal." She hears a door close upstairs and speeds up. "And that is all it is, a political view. He's your husband, no matter what has been said or done. I think you should just visit him, just once. Who knows, seeing you might bring him out of having any foolish ideas of killing himself on a hunger strike."

The last bit was genius and Mary is pleased. She's done what she can to keep her end of the bargain to get Bronwyn to go and visit her husband. She sneaks a sideways look at her. She appears deep in thought. Mary nods to herself and hopes she has done enough.

Chapter 13

February 22nd 1981

There were more maggots this morning. The ones that came first, days ago, are flies now. I don't know which ones are worse. The flies, I think. At least the maggots just stay where you fling them. The flies are enough to induce a mental breakdown, buzzing around all day and all night.

I can hear the breakfast trays being removed. The guards hate coming down this block. The maggots and the flies and the excrement on the walls are too much for them. To my surprise, I've almost got used to the smell of shit and piss. A priest came around yesterday and spoke to us all. I've never seen a man try so hard not to vomit before. His face was puce with the effort of holding it all inside.

"Visitor, Granger," shouted one of the screws as he banged on my bars.

I sit up and then stand, the cold and my situation all but forgotten. She's here. *Finally.*

I traipse along behind the guard, wrapping my blanket around me, responding to the calls and greetings of my fellow prisoners. I stop at Sean's cell, exchange a few words, until the screw barks back down the corridor.

"I'll send your visitor away, then, shall I?"

Sean gestures at me to go, and I wink at him and stroll after the screw. You can't hurry in here, you can't make them think they have control. Every single thing you say or do has to be thought out in advance.

We reach a door, one of the visiting rooms, and the screw silently opens it. I saunter in.

My visitor is there.

It's Bronwyn.

I walk around the room and come to a stop in front of her. I let her look at me, at the blanket and my lack of clothes. Even though I've got used to it I know she can smell my cell on me. Slowly her eyes travel from my bare feet, all the way up my body until her eyes lock onto mine.

"For fuck's sake," she hisses.

I smile, give her a bit of the old me, but inside I'm struggling. Now she's here I don't know what to say. Since I've been banged up I've had so many conversations with her in my head. Now that she sits in front of me, my speech has deserted me.

"You look well," I say, as I take my seat. Even though it's a lie; she looks tired and too skinny. Bronwyn was never skinny. She was muscled with an athlete's build. She was strong and solid but always feminine. And it crosses my mind that this is the first time I've properly looked at her in years.

"You look like shit, and you smell like it too."

In spite of her words I grin again. My wife is back.

"So, you're doing it then?"

"Yes, I am." I'm proud and I make sure she knows it.

"Jesus Christ, Dan, I didn't think even you would be so stupid."

Her tone and her words anger me and I lean forward, I put my face right up to hers.

"It's not stupid, don't you ever call me stupid."

She doesn't recoil from me, and I applaud her for that. I would have.

She doesn't say anything else. She slumps in her chair and looks down at the floor.

"What did you come for, Bron?" I ask her, gently this time.

She shrugs her shoulders, suddenly twenty years younger.

I can see tears are pooling in her eyes and I frown. A little of what I used to feel breathes inside me and I'm asking myself, what happened? How did I – we – get here? And I can't allow myself to reminisce about years gone by. I've got a different goal now, I've got a job to do, an important one, and my people are now those men who sit in their cells behind me. They are my family now.

"I went to the forest the other day," she says, and looks up at me. "You know, where we used to go when we first got the house."

I can't read her expression, not through her tears.

"I wanted to collect some stones and rocks, I wanted something solid to commemorate Emma, and I had to get stones because I haven't got anything else solid in my life. Not anymore."

I scratch my belly underneath the itchy blanket. My skin seems to have got so much more sensitive since I've not bathed.

"Who the fuck is Emma?" I ask. I'm lost, I don't remember any of her friends who are called Emma. Not that I know many of them, she never seems to have any mates, only the irritating Rose constantly hanging around.

"Emma was our baby," she says, looking me straight in the eye. "I lost a baby, Danny."

Her tears have stopped, which is one good thing. I don't know how she wants me to respond and it's obvious that she expects a response.

I scratch again, my back this time, and wonder absentmindedly if I've got one of the damn maggots stuck to me.

"Are you going to say anything?" Her voice goes up a notch and she's almost shrill.

I smile, I shrug, I answer her honestly. "I don't... what do you want me to say, Bron?"

She stands up and walks behind me, out of view. I wait for her to speak, because if I know her she's got plenty more to say. There's a small noise, I swing around in my chair.

The room is empty.

My wife has gone.

*

Bronwyn holds her tears in check all the way home on the bus. She stares out of the window at the rolling countryside and looks at none of the other passengers. She thinks of the couple of tins of Guinness that she bought home from Mary's and closes her eyes at the thought of the taste. She will open it as soon as she gets home. She will not have any lunch or dinner and if she finishes off the beer she will go out and get more.

The plan helps, knowing what she will be doing makes the bus journey a little easier. At the bus stop she gets off, hurrying now towards Kidds Road. Now she has made a plan that will make her forget about everything, she can't wait to put it into action.

When she opens the door she flings her bag onto the carpet and makes for the kitchen. To her horror, Alia is there, and she has opened one of the cans of beer.

"What are you doing?" Bronwyn shouts, before she can stop herself.

"Calm down, Bronwyn!" Her mother's volume matches her own.

Bronwyn grabs the can and holds it close to her chest. "It's mine!"

She hears her words and how childish they sound, but really, this beer, it was all that was keeping her going, all the way home, the thought of getting good and blotted so she wouldn't have to think of Danny's words, how callous he was, how he didn't even care about Emma.

She hears a gasp, realises that it came from her, from somewhere deep within and she's breathing in, gasping, until she can't hold it anymore and a scream comes out of her, wracking her body until her legs don't work and she goes down into a kneeling position right there, on the kitchen floor, losing all power in her limbs, except the ability to hold onto the can of Guinness, still clamped against her breasts.

*

Alia had known that Bronwyn was getting somewhere close to breaking point, but she hadn't expected the scene that is playing out before her. For a horrible moment she thinks about getting up and leaving, because she's never seen Bronwyn like this, so out of control, so emotional. But to leave would mean stepping over her daughter's crumpled body, and she couldn't do that to anyone, let alone her own flesh and blood.

Still she doesn't move, one hand is still clasping her glass as she stares down at Bronwyn. In between the sobs she makes out a single word.

"Ma...,"

It galvanises her into action, and she puts the glass on the table, tips forward off her chair and lands on her knees next to Bronwyn.

Yes, I'm a mother, this is my girl, my only child, thinks Alia. *But this child has never needed me, not since she learned how to walk, so forgive me if my reactions are slow. And, oh my God, but it's so good to be needed, finally, at last...*

Later they talk about it, over a bottle of wine that Alia found buried in the back of the cupboard underneath the kitchen sink and which Bronwyn had missed. They go through to the living room and Alia, still with Bronwyn in her arms, switches on the electric fire. They sink onto the sofa, sip at their wine, and eventually Bronwyn begins to talk, about Danny mostly. Alia listens without interrupting, nodding occasionally, even when Bronwyn's sentences run into one another and don't make any sense. She hears a lot about Emma, whoever she is, and interjects about how everyone knows that she grassed on Danny, punctuated with crying jags and swear words.

"I waited all your life for you to need me," Alia says, a little drunk now. "You never did, today is the first time you have ever needed me like that."

She watches for Bronwyn's reaction. Bronwyn shakes her head and raises her hands, palms up. "I never really needed anything, ma. Everything was always manageable, until recently."

Manageable, not okay, Alia, even though she's not sober, notices the word her daughter chooses to use.

Bronwyn starts up again, omitting nothing; about how over the years Dan has been getting in deeper and deeper, staying out later and later, until they barely see each other and don't talk.

"He doesn't need me, ma," Bronwyn says, and her voice breaks Alia's heart. "He didn't want to hear about Emma either, you know he's on the protests?"

Alia puts her hand to her mouth, remembering how bad it had got last winter. Something else pokes at her through the alcohol haze. "You keep talking about... Emma?"

Bronwyn smiles, almost looks happy for a second. "I named her Emma, ma."

Alia nods, says nothing in reply, but pulls Bronwyn close to her. "Do you want to come and stay with me for a bit?"

Bronwyn pulls away and shakes her head no. "Thanks, but I'll be fine." She looks down, almost shyly, and Alia tugs at her hand.

"What?"

Bronwyn looks up at her mother, her eyes wide and almost hopeful. "I thought I might start running again, I miss it, you know?"

"I don't think it'll solve anything, you're just running away from your problems, soft girl."

Bronwyn shrugs. "Better than sitting staring at them in the bottom of a glass."

As Alia goes to leave, she feels a little better. Sometimes things just have to come to a head, and today, they did.

"See you, ma," says Bronwyn. "Thank you... for everything."

And as Alia walks back to her own house, she smiles, suddenly, as she realises something. Bronwyn has called her 'ma' more times in a few hours today than she has in the last decade.

*

You need to make an effort.

You need to make an effort.

Connor's words to Rose of the night before play in her head, over and over.

After she had seen Bronwyn arrive she had taken a moment to gather herself before going downstairs. At the time she hadn't known why she would need to take that time, after all, Bronwyn was her lifelong best friend. She hadn't thought too much about it, just sat down on the bed for a moment to prepare herself. She could hear them in the kitchen when she went down and she hovered in the gloom of the hallway. They hadn't seen her, though she could see Mary moving around in the kitchen. She saw Mary get three plates out and carry them across the room, and as she had passed the open door she had nudged it closed.

Three plates for the three people seated at the table.

It's like I don't exist, thought Rose as she slowly climbed back upstairs. *It's as though Bronwyn is Connor's girlfriend and she's come round for tea.*

Later, much later, Connor had come up to the room.

"Bronwyn's bought some cans," he had said, his face flushed by the good time they were having downstairs without her. "Come and have a drink."

Rose had shaken her head.

He had looked at her for a long moment. And then he had spoken those words that pierced through her heart.

"You need to make an effort."

He had gone back down and Rose had waited patiently for Bronwyn to come up and see her. She would, wouldn't she? After all, it was Rose that Bronwyn had come to visit, seeing as she barely knew Mary or Connor.

But Bronwyn hadn't come upstairs, and when Rose heard movement in the hallway she had gone to the window and peered out into the darkness. In the pale light of the street lamp, Rose saw it was Mary who was seeing Bronwyn out. They spoke for a minute, Mary seemed to be doing most of the talking, Bronwyn nodding her head, before they parted with a wave.

Rose had crawled under her covers, shaking even though the room was warm. Mary had never spoken to Rose like that, in fact she barely spoke to her at all.

This morning Rose had worked up the courage to mention that fact to Connor. He was getting ready for work, pulling on his thickest jumper.

"I tell you, I'm warmer when I working outside doing the bricks, I swear they don't believe in having the heating on in the office, tight bastards," he was grumbling.

"Did your mum get on okay with Bronwyn?" Rose asked, as she stood in the doorway of his bedroom. She wasn't going to go in, she'd learned her lesson on that subject.

"Yeah, they had a nice night, I think," he said, reaching over to grab a second pair of socks to put on before twisting around to look at her. "Why?"

"She doesn't really talk to me, your mother, I mean."

He had seemed almost angry as he wadded the socks into a ball and threw them in the general direction of the chest of drawers.

"Maybe she feels the same about you," he said. "Why don't you try *talking* to her?"

He had left then, giving her upper arm a squeeze as he limped past her. She waited until she heard the front door close and leaned against the doorframe. He didn't even kiss her goodbye, never before had they parted company with him simply pressing his hand to her arm.

She heard the clock radio come to life in Mary's bedroom and Rose hurried down the stairs. If Connor wanted her to make an effort she would.

She gets the good teabags out of the cupboard, from behind the rows of cans where she knows Mary stashes them. There's half a loaf left over from the day before, and an unopened jar of locally produced jam. She busies herself, waiting until she hears Mary go into the bathroom and once she can hear the immersion heater gurgling away in the upstairs airing cupboard, she starts to prepare breakfast for Mary.

Ten minutes later there are footsteps on the stairs, and when Mary doesn't come into the kitchen Rose opens the door.

Mary is in the hallway, winding her scarf around her neck.

"I... I made you a pot of tea," Rose stutters. "And some toast."

Mary looks over at her. To Rose it seems she is about to speak, when she presses her lips firmly together and reaches for her coat. Without a single word, Mary pulls open the front door, retrieves her handbag from where it hangs on the banister, and walks stiffly outside.

Rose gapes as the door closes behind Mary. She can smell the toast under the grill and she stalks back into the kitchen and pulls out the tray. The bread is charred and blackened and the handle is hot. She flings it into the sink with a cry and sits down at the table to examine her fingers.

A silver mark has appeared between her thumb and forefinger and she knows it will blister later. She stares at the cuts on her palm from the smashed glass the other evening. With a sob caught in her throat she places her wrist against the teapot, not flinching, but relishing the heat even as her skin screams a message to her brain telling her to stop. As she holds her arm there, her sleeve rides up a little, showing the scratches that she made without consciously thinking the night before, with the letter opener.

*

Mary has nowhere to go, but she had heard Rose clattering mugs and plates in the kitchen and knew that the girl would be preparing food for her. She had hid in the bathroom for as long as was acceptable. It niggled at her though, the fact that she was hiding in her own home. She's lived here for over two decades with Connor, just the two of them, and neither of them have ever hidden from each other. Her home has always been a sanctuary, a shelter away from the troubles outside, a place of occasional laughter and always love along with rest and relaxation.

This isn't the first time that she has seen Connor with a girl, of course it isn't, he is in his twenties, after all. But before she could see them for what they were; an endless parade of short-skirted, big-breasted tarts - good for passing the time over a couple of weeks or a month. And she never begrudged him that, because he was a good looking, red-blooded man, and because he always returned to her, to his mother, the only woman that should ever really matter in a man's life. Never has she let one stay in her home before though, and she can't quite believe that Rose is ensconced in her house. It's dangerous, the longer she stays here, the more chance there is of further attacks.

But this Rose, there is something troubling about her. Mary has thought about it a lot since she learned of the girl's existence on the night of the shooting. It's the plainness of her, with all of the others their intentions and wishes were obvious, there for all to see in their straining bras and painted on their faces along with the slick of lipstick. Because there is nothing obvious in Rose's exterior, Mary has come to the conclusion there must be something inside her, something very special that is hidden away, not to be noticed by just looking at her. Why else would Connor risk his life by seeing her, and expect his mother to put her up in their home?

She can't spend another day with her in the house, skirting around each other, giving side glances and living in awkward silences. When Connor goes to work Mary likes to listen to the radio and potter around the house, not hide in the bathroom, constantly on her guard.

Mary had checked her reflection in the mirror before exiting the bathroom. She tried to walk quietly downstairs and in the hallway she snatched up her scarf. The kitchen door opened and Rose's anxious face appeared, talking about tea and toast.

Mary had been about to reply, to make an excuse that she had to be somewhere but she stopped herself. She needed to up her game, needed to make the girl feel as uncomfortable as possible, so without a word she had put on her coat and walked out of the front door without a backward glance.

She doesn't have anywhere to be, she has no friends to speak of that she can call on, and as the cold bites at her she is furious that Rose is left in the nice, warm home and it's her, Mary, turfed out and tramping the streets of Newry.

She starts walking, away from the park and towards the quay area. It only takes ten minutes and she finds herself alongside the church of Saint Mary. Outside the gates she grips onto the gold topped black railings and looks through into the graveyard. It's not her church, hers is Saint Patrick's, rumoured to be the first Protestant church built in Ireland. But though this one in front of her is Catholic, she prefers it to her own place of worship, because this is where Billy is. She doesn't come here much, other people seem to find it a comfort to have a marker for their loved ones. Not Mary, she's never seen it that way. Connor is her marker for the love she lost, not some slab of marble. But she's here now, and she pushes open the gate and walks past the church, past the graves of the war dead until she stands over the burial site of Billy Dean, Connor's father.

There is no mention of their son on the headstone, nor the fact that Billy was a father. Of course there wouldn't be, he didn't know that she was pregnant when he died. Mary will never forget when she came to his funeral, staying at a respectable distance until all of the other mourners had melted away and she had finally gathered up enough courage to approach Billy's parents. They were bereft in their grief, barely listening to her as she explained who she was, and what Billy had been to her. They had turned away, Billy's father's arm encasing his wife, and Mary had understood, it was all too much, she shouldn't have done this on the day they buried their son. She left it another six weeks and this time went to their home. It turned out they had heard her words on the day of the funeral, but they shunned her, they chose to ignore her existence and the impending arrival of their only grandchild. She never went to them again and once, she had been in the town centre with Connor and she had seen the mother. Connor was two years old, toddling along, and Mary had seen Billy's mother first. Instinct told Mary to pick up her son and walk in the other direction, but her heart told her not to. That had surprised her, since the death of Billy and the abandonment of his folk, she had thought her heart was dead but it appeared not. She held little Connor's hand tight and with her head high she walk past Billy's mother, fixing her with a stare that was so intense the older woman couldn't fail to notice it, to feel it.

Mary had offered her a look which she hoped conveyed everything she meant it to. *Look at him*, she thought, *look at your grandson. See how much he looks like his father? See what you're missing out on by ignoring this piece of your son?*

She hoped it had worked; she fervently sent a wish that the older Mrs Dean recognised her as the woman who had come begging at her door. She wondered if they ever knew that she had taken their son's name. Probably, things didn't stay secret around here.

Now, over twenty years have passed and never again had she seen Billy's parents. They would probably be dead now, and for that she is irrationally envious, jealous that they get to see Billy again before she does.

And as she crouches in front of Billy's headstone she wonders what would happen if events repeated themselves, and Rose was having a baby. It would be an absolute disaster, and she must not let it get that far. She wonders now if she has more in common with Billy's parents than any of them ever thought, and suddenly she understands a little of how they must have felt. She rocks back, sits down properly on the damp grass and grips her chest as her heart thuds heavily inside her. How ironic that now, twenty-three years later, she is not seeing the black and white, but all the shades of grey in between.

Chapter 14

February 23rd 1981

When Bronwyn returns from her run she staggers up to the front door on legs that have only started shaking now she has slowed to a walk. Her throat is dry, her breath rasping and despite the dull ache starting in her calves she feels good. A good sort of tired and all she wants is a pint glass filled with water. There will be no wine today.

She almost changes her mind about the alcohol when she pushes the front door open and sees the envelopes marked with red writing that have been put through the letterbox. In bold print, three of them declare that they are final reminders. She picks them up, takes them through to the kitchen and sitting down at the table she carefully opens them. There is one from the T.V rental company, an electricity bill and a demand for payment of the gas. Final reminders though, that means letters have been sent before but she is certain she hasn't seen any unpaid bills. It's her priority, the one single thing she takes pride in, paying her bills when they come in the post.

Danny must have taken them before she saw them, and she swears softly. She should have known, after all it's been at least a month that he's been unemployed. Things have been tight for a long time but now she's the only one living in the house, she is going to have to shape up. Vaguely she recalls her mother asking if she was okay for money the other day, and she knows that she can ask her, but she doesn't want to rely on a handout. And if Dan isn't coming back anytime soon then she needs to take care of herself.

Alia had a newspaper yesterday, a local one, maybe she should be looking at the classifieds. Pushing the bills to one side she looks around the downstairs of the house, finally locating the copy of *The Newry Reporter* down the side of the sofa in the living room. She flicks to the job page, grabs a pen and takes the paper back to the kitchen. It's cleaning jobs, mostly, actually what seems like an abundance of them. Housekeeping she can do, and she circles half a dozen of them. She'll make the calls now, she decides, while she's still got her trainers on, and gathering up some coins and taking the newspaper with her, she jogs down to the phone box.

One of them, a Mr McKeown, head of Windsor Hill Primary School, asks if she could pop along this morning. Bronwyn looks down at her tracksuit and runs her hand through her hair which was definitely in need of a wash. Then she thinks of the red bills and grips the phone tight.

"I can make it by 10 o'clock, if that's okay?"

It was, and she hangs up and runs back to the house, not bothering to phone any of the other advertisements. It's too far to walk to make it in time, so after a frantically fast hair wash and bath Bronwyn checks the bus timetable that is pinned up on the kitchen wall. There's a bus at half nine, and Bronwyn checks her watch as she runs upstairs to check her wardrobe. Standing wrapped in the bath towel she surveys her clothes. There is nothing suitable for a job interview, even if it is just for a cleaning position. She hasn't had cause to wear clothes like that for years.

"I could so easily forget this and go and buy a bottle instead," she mutters to herself.

She digs out a suit, eventually. It's her funeral outfit, last worn at Dan's mother's wake three years ago. They nearly hadn't gone, after being shuffled between foster homes and child care services all through his childhood, the death of his mother hadn't been a great loss or a huge shock. Bronwyn shivers standing in her towel as she remembers the tall, thin woman who had abused herself for decades with gin and street drugs. The only surprise had been that she lived as long as she did.

It is a memory she shouldn't have allowed herself, because it always causes her a pang of sympathy for Danny. She couldn't imagine growing up without the constant presence of Alia. And it had been Alia who raised him, really, actually, all three of them; Bronwyn, Dan and Rose. Always, even though Alia herself was a single mother, she always seemed to have enough food to make sure Bronwyn and her two friends got at least one hot meal a day. And Alia's love had been all that Bronwyn needed, why couldn't it have been enough for Danny? Why did he feel the need to spend his youth and his twenties chasing after the older men, seeking validation and a sense of belonging?

She pulls on the suit, wrinkling her nose at her reflection as she grasps the spare material at the front of the trousers. The last time she had worn this she hadn't been as skinny as she is now.

She looks at the clock on the nightstand. The time is getting on, and she hurries downstairs, nerves mingled with a shimmer of excitement at the thought of moving on.

*

Though it seems to Rose like time has stopped, she knows it hasn't. It takes her a while but finally she works out that Mary has been gone for almost two hours. The grill tray is still in the sink, the toast, black and cold. The kitchen is a mess with the butter out on the worktop, slowly softening, and the jam alongside it. The teapot is cold now and the kitchen table is smudged with blood.

Rose pushes herself up and shuffles over to the sink. She washes the blood off her own arm first, and then scrubs at the red stain on the paring knife. She moves the grill and the old pieces of toast, and as she fills up the sink she hears a knock at the front door.

Rose freezes, stands stock still with her hands in the soapy water. Her hands and wrist sting, jolting her and she yanks her arms up, away from the water, and wipes them on the tea towel. Blood traces are left on the towel but she barely notices as she moves into the hall.

The front door is opaque glass, impossible to see through, and Rose begins to shake as she notices a dark shape outside in the porch. The letterbox rattles as it is opened roughly, and then, Rose hears her name.

It's Bronwyn, just Bronwyn. Rose opens the door, blinks at her friend.

"Gosh, you look smart," Rose says. "Are you coming in?"

"I had a job interview, just cleaning at the school, but I need to work, I'm broke," Bronwyn says as she takes in Rose's appearance. "What happened to you?"

Rose looks down at the red stained towel. "I had an accident," she murmurs. "Do you want to come through?"

Bronwyn follows her through and as they stand in the kitchen, she snatches Rose's hands up in her own. "How many accidents did you have?"

Rose pulls out of Bronwyn's grasp, moves to the sink and turns off the still running tap. She can feel the heat in her face as she yanks her sleeves down over her hands. "It doesn't matter," she replies, her tone dull and almost sulky.

Bronwyn flings her bag onto the table, narrowly missing the trails of blood.

"You done this to yourself, I know you, I know exactly what happens when you feel this way."

Rose rubs at her eyes, she's so tired. It's not even lunchtime and she hasn't exactly had a busy morning, but she feels so weary.

"And why are you not at work?" snaps Bronwyn. "Have you even called them? If you're not careful you'll end up like me, red bills piling up and out looking for cleaning jobs."

"I don't have any bills," Rose says the words without thinking, only realising how they sound when she catches sight of Bronwyn's furious expression.

"Well, aren't you the lucky one?" Bronwyn crosses her arms and leans back against the counter. "Aren't we just miss lady-of-the-manor?"

"Oh, Bron, I didn't mean it like that," Rose cries as she reaches for Bronwyn.

Bronwyn lurches away, coming to sit in the chair that Rose had vacated only minutes earlier. There is an uneasy silence, until Bronwyn speaks up.

"Sorry about all that business about your Dad," she says. "It must have been horrible for you."

Rose has known Bronwyn long enough to know that she is trying for an apology, but her breath catches in her throat. "How did you know? Did Mary tell you?"

"No, Connor did, the other day…," Bronwyn tails off and Rose knows her face is aflame again.

Connor knows? So why hasn't he mentioned it to her? Does he not think it's a big deal, or does he not even care? She is sinking, she is in such a big hole and there just doesn't seem to be any way of digging herself out of it. Worse than that, she can't find the energy to try and pull herself out. Maybe it's best to stay in the hole, out of everyone's way. And one day, someone might come along and fill in the hole, piling earth on top of her and she'll just be there, quiet, gone away and no more bother to anybody.

She puts her hands in her lap and scratches at a scab forming on the underside of her wrist. It's not ready to come off, the scab, it's too new, too fresh, but she accepts the pain, willingly and gratefully. She lets it take over, it's better than having to listen to Bronwyn sniping at her. And then Bronwyn is standing over her, pulling her arms and Rose gapes at her strength. She struggles against her, twisting in her seat.

"Stop it," Bronwyn shouts as she grapples for Rose's arms. "For Christ's sake, what's wrong with you?"

Rose slumps and Bronwyn's grip relaxes.

"What do you think is wrong with me?" Rose hears her voice, loud – for once, not meek and subservient as she usually is.

"You're not the only one!" Bronwyn shouts. "How do you think I've been, I've lost everything, my husband, Emma – it's all gone!"

Rose's mouth forms the word as a question, "Emma?" But before either of them can speak the front door is slammed closed and Mary sweeps down the hall into the kitchen.

"What the hell is going on, I can hear you from outside!"

Rose looks around, sees clearly for the first time what Mary is looking at. The plates and the grill pan, the butter and jam and the knives, all strewn over the worktop and table. And the blood, on the tea towel, on the table near Bronwyn's bag, on Rose's sleeves.

"I should go," says Bronwyn.

Mary looks over at her, as if seeing her for the first time. "I'll walk you out," she says, stiffly.

Rose watches them, as both the women stare at her for a long moment. Mary, angry, yet again and Bronwyn, her expression seems worse, like Rose has let her down.

Chapter 15

"I'll walk a little way with you," says Mary to Bronwyn as they go down the front path.

She has been out all morning, sitting in the cold by Billy's grave, but she can't go back inside yet. Hopefully when she returns Rose's mess will have been cleared up. Anger is thumping inside her chest, she can't believe the girl is so useless that she can't even use the kitchen without turning it into a warzone. And what was all that blood about? Rose is an accident-prone witch. Mary looks sidelong at Bronwyn and silently appraises the woman. Not for the first time she wonders how they are still friends. It's common in childhood, she knows that, there is usually a leader and a follower, but for this unlikely pair to still be close in adulthood is strange.

"Did you visit your husband?" Mary asks, remembering why she had decided to walk out with Bronwyn.

"Yeah, for all the good it did," replies Bronwyn, sullenly, before looking up at Mary. "You were right, you know, he's on the blanket protest."

Mary nods, gives Bronwyn what she hopes is a sympathetic look. "Are you off to see his solicitor or something, all togged up?"

Bronwyn emits a laugh, short and sharp. "No, I have to get a job if I want to keep my home."

Another difference between Bronwyn and Rose, thinks Mary. One has a perfectly decent job yet doesn't bother to go to work, and this one sees her own situation and is doing what she needs to in order to improve her own life. Mary stops walking, Bronwyn, not noticing, carries on.

"I'll see you later," Mary says softly.

Bronwyn doesn't halt or turn, and Mary wonders if she even heard her speak or noticed that Mary was no longer walking alongside her.

Mary crosses over the street, makes a phone call via the operator and then heads towards the bus stop. If Bronwyn has been to see Danny then Mary has done her job. Now Danny Granger needs to stick to his end of the bargain.

After an hour she finds herself once again at Long Kesh. There are a lot more people than last time, but they seem to be hanging around the gates and some of them look like television reporters. She desperately wants to light up a cigarette, but knows it's not wise to linger out here. She puts her head down, sinks her chin into her scarf and makes her way quickly to the entrance. She has to wait longer than last time, and she sits in the communal room, her bag on her lap, not watching the people who sit alongside, who also don't talk to her.

Finally her name is called and she travels down the same corridor, following the guard, pulling her scarf up around her nose and mouth to try and dispel the horrid aroma that seems to seep out of the cells.

He is already in the cell-like room when they show her in, sitting, facing away from her, the blanket pulled tightly around him. She stops just inside the door, even with her coat and scarf and gloves she can still feel the chill. He must be freezing. He hasn't turned around yet and Mary is grateful for the time it gives her. This man could be her son, sitting here, naked save for a prison issue blanket. Prepared to be bone cold, prepared to go without food, preparing for die. But like the seed of fondness she almost felt for Bronwyn, she mentally pummels it down. She can't sympathise with these people, they are not her people and especially this man in front of her, the one that shot her son through his leg, she can't feel anything for any of them.

"She came then," she says, her voice ringing around the small room.

He doesn't turn around, forcing her to walk in front of him. She swallows hard and hopes the horror doesn't show on her face.

He looks up at her with tired, bloodshot eyes. His hands, indeed his whole body, from what she can see, are filthy, smudged with brown dirt and his feet are caked with grime and grit.

"I'm actually looking forward to the hunger strike," he says, by way of explanation for his appearance.

"You're mad." Mary sits down opposite him, taking care that his legs don't touch her skirt. "I can't believe anyone would willingly do this to themselves."

He doesn't reply, and she picks at an imaginary piece of lint on her coat. She didn't come here to talk politics, that doesn't interest her, and she has more important things on her mind.

"So, I kept the deal, I got Bronwyn to come and see you. Now you do your part."

He shifts on the chair and she feels another rush of unexpected pity as he tucks the blanket underneath him.

"What do you want?" he asks.

How quickly emotions can change, a small part of her mind notes this as his tone, almost insolent, causes the pity to dissipate and a rush of annoyance takes its place. She leans forward, points her finger at him.

"You know what I want, I want the girl gone. I want her out of my house and my life, and out of my son's life, too."

He looks like he's pondering this fact and she stifles a sigh. He's playing with her, he is holding the cards and he knows it. And she can't afford to lose her temper because he could simply laugh and not accept any more visits from her. He has nothing to lose.

The silence is long and the room is suddenly so quiet that Mary can hear the ticking of the clock on the far wall. She thinks back to this morning, of how she had to get out of her own house – twice, and the mess in the kitchen and the blood that stained the table and Rose's sleeves. She hasn't really focussed on the blood, dare not ask herself what happened, what the girl had been doing to herself. Because it wasn't an accident, Mary isn't so out of touch that she thinks any of Rose's strange wounds are accidental. And she can't have that in her home, because how long before Rose totally loses control and turns her knives and weapons on someone else in the household? She snaps her head away from the ticking clock and leans forward. Ignoring the grime and the smell, she grasps Danny's bare knee. He looks up, surprised.

"You need to help me, I will do anything I can for you in return, do you understand?"

It's as though those were the words he was waiting for and he lifts an eyebrow, smiles lopsided at her. In that moment she can see the man he was before the politics took him over. A man not unlike her own son, cheeky, good-looking: a skirt-chaser and a jack-the-lad. She has to remind herself what this man in front of her has done to her son. She has to remind herself that he held her Connor down on the ground and cold heartedly put a bullet through his leg. It's hard when she is in the room with this one, though, when she sees him, cold and alone and surely frightened, even if he doesn't show it. She tries to step it up a little, when her anger fades, by imagining this is the man who killed her Billy. Who knows, it was maybe even a bloodline of Danny, an uncle or a cousin, even his father.

"I'd like to see my wife again," he says and clears his throat. "I don't think I said the right words last time, I was sideswiped, I didn't know about the miscarriage and I didn't handle it very well. I didn't even get to talk to her about grassing me up to the police. So yes, make her come here again, and I'll get rid of your problem."

This time she lets her sigh escape, unchecked. She had been afraid of that, as far as Mary was concerned it was the hardest thing she had done, and it would be even more difficult now, if Rose and Bronwyn had had a row, which to Mary it seemed they did this morning. There is less chance of Bronwyn coming round the house for Mary to try and convince her to come here again.

Then she thinks of this morning, the state of the kitchen, the horrible atmosphere that Rose drags around the home with her, wearing it like a shawl, and Mary raises her chin.

"I'll try my best," she says to Danny and fixes him with a stare. "But you need to sort out my little problem right away, there's no waiting until your wife comes in here."

"How do I know you'll even talk to my wife?" he fires back.

"You'll have to trust me," replies Mary.

He looks like he is about to thank her, he actually looks grateful, but Mary can't let their relationship go that far, that's not what this is all about, after all. She stands, quickly, and backs away from him, walks a wide arc around him, still seated in his pathetic blanket, to the door.

"When did this miscarriage happen?" she asks, her mind only now registering his words now that her own issues are dealt with.

"She reckons she lost a baby," he says, hoarsely.

Don't walk back to him, just leave it, she tells herself. *This is nothing to do with you, this is getting into the dangerous territory of actually caring.* But oh God, it's so hard not to walk over to him and fold him in her arms, just to offer a bit of humanity. And the urge surprises Mary, she's not a natural comforter, she doesn't offer up hugs and sympathy like many women her own age do.

She takes a last look around the room, looks at the back of the young man. It's terrible, this room, this whole place. She hopes that this is the last time she sets foot in Long Kesh, and the last time she claps eyes on Danny Granger.

*

Bronwyn pulls off the suit as soon as she gets home. Dragging on a pair of well-worn jeans and a jumper she goes downstairs and puts the fire on in the kitchen.

Mr McKeown had offered her the job, right there on the spot after chatting for fifteen minutes. She had felt almost lightheaded with relief after being scared that he was going to judge her, that he had heard that she had grassed up her own husband's activities. But perhaps Mr McKeown didn't move in those sort of circles, or maybe he just didn't care what sort of woman he employed to clean his school.

"Perhaps we can see how you go, and if anything else comes up, maybe a position in the library...," He had said, almost apologetic that she was going to be employed as a cleaner.

A job in the library doesn't interest her, cleaning is about all she can manage right now, and only because it comes naturally and without having to think about the task in hand. She didn't say this though, she just nodded politely.

She will commence work tomorrow, she can wear jeans and a jumper and she has already been given a tabard and her own peg in the cloakroom. She will start work at 7 o'clock in the morning. On the way home she checked the bus timetable. There is a bus that goes that early, but she is thinking now that she could incorporate her morning run into her new routine and she could jog to work. She could put her jeans in one of Danny's old rucksacks and change when she reaches the school. She wouldn't have to change out of her trainers, they would do to work in. And then when she finishes the cleaning duties at about half eight she could run home again, all her work done and dusted by 9 o'clock.

She smiles, thinks of Mr McKeown and his kindness. She's not sure if he knows that her husband is in prison. Probably, everybody knows everything in this place. He surely doesn't know that she put Danny inside though, or he wouldn't have been so quick to offer her the job.

She shivers, the electric fire isn't warming her. It's burning her legs in patches, but she's still so cold. Bronwyn opens the cupboard underneath the sink and retrieves her hairdryer. Plugging it in and switching it on she puts it underneath her jumper. Instant relief. She smiles fondly as she recalls her and Alia doing this very thing years ago. When you're poor you learn any tricks to keep you warm. The cold was worse than hunger, because for some reason people thought eating was more important than being warm. Alia would send Bronwyn to the local fish and chip shop some evenings and she would push some shillings over the counter, asking for as many chips as she could get with the amount she had. Always, without fail, the kindly servers would hand her over a full portion.

She considers breaking further into her cash and treating herself to fish and chips to celebrate her new job. Turning off the hairdryer she grabs a couple of pounds and pulls her coat back on.

Later, the cod and chips gone and with a warm, full belly, her thoughts turn to Danny. There will be no nipping to the chippie for him, and on the blanket protest he'll be cold to the bone.

It's the first time she's thought of him in ages without a stab of something that is close to hate. She shakes the feeling off and turns over the television channel to take her mind off him.

It works for a while as she sinks into *Wish You Were Here*, which just makes her sad that she can't see a time in her future where she would be able to have a holiday like the ones on the television. She flips over to *Hart to Hart*, but finding that she can't follow the story she switches the set off.

Shuffling into the kitchen she digs around in the bin for the bottle of wine that Alia had opened. She pops the cork, washes the mug that held her earlier coffee and fills it up. As she sits back down in front of the fire she slowly sips at the wine, all the while thinking about Danny.

*

Rose ensured that the kitchen was as clean as a whistle by the time Mary returned. She used bleach and scouring pads, threw away the ruined toast and washed up every cup, plate and utensil that she had used.

It helped; while she was busy she wasn't thinking and by the time she has finished she has worked up enough of a sweat that she pulls her jumper off and stands in her T-shirt.

Perhaps I can do more, she thinks, *maybe I can make an effort*. She takes a bowl of warm water into the lounge and the bleach bottle. She examines the room. It's already tidy, really, but she can see rings on the wooden coffee table where someone has placed a mug without a coaster.

With a softer sponge she squirts on the bleach, pleased to see the ring disappear. She does the whole table top, carefully moving Mary's garish lady ornament out of the way.

She scrubs harder at an obstinate stain, pushing down on the sponge so much that her fingers lock up at the knuckles. She lets go of the sponge, rubs her hand, feeling the pain of the cleaning fluid in her cuts now she's lost her concentration.

Tears unexpectedly fill her eyes and she pulls her T-shirt up at the bottom, rubs her face with it. As she leans back on her heels there is a blurry shape, moving so fast that she falls backwards, landing awkwardly on her left hip, grasping out at the table to keep her balance. She lets out a cry, looks up, but doesn't feel relief when she sees that it's just Mary, towering over her.

"What are you doing?" Mary's cry is a plaintive wail.

What did I do now? Rose looks around, trying to find out the source of Mary's obvious anger. "I-I'm cleaning," she stammers.

Mary snatches up the bottle of bleach and thrusts it in Rose's face. "Not with this! You don't use this on wood, it's a bloody antique and it's *ruined*!"

Rose jerks backwards as a fine spray of bleach flicks from the top over Rose's face. Before she can respond, Mary lets out another shout of horror and gazes down to the floor. Rose follows her gaze, sees the sponge, wet with bleach, face down on the navy blue carpet.

"Everything you touch turns to SHITE!" shouts Mary and Rose can see her hands shaking so violently that bleach is spitting out now, covering everything within a couple of feet.

She's going to hit me, she's going to kill me, thinks Rose. But the thought is processed calmly, and this showdown, though horrible, is almost welcome. She sits on her behind on the floor, heart beating almost audibly, waiting for the inevitable slap or punch. She can feel something wet on her face and she doesn't know if it's the bleach, Mary's spittle, or even her own tears.

Hit me, she begs silently, *give me a good black eye so I can show your son what you did to me, and then maybe he'll take me away out of this house of horrors.*

But Mary stands motionless, her chest heaving, her breathing loud. Still wanting something, the smallest movement that Rose can take as a threat she moves her right leg out straight and purposefully brushes Mary's ankle, provoking a reaction.

Mary looks down sharply, walks a couple of steps backwards and looks directly at Rose.

"You need to get out," she says, her voice still loud but not quite a shout. "I can't have you here, I can't live like this."

Rose doesn't reply but some spark of tyranny must come back to Mary, and with a rebel yell she winds back her arm and throws the bottle of bleach at Rose. Her reactions are slow, non-existent really, and the bottom of the bottle hits her square in the middle of her face. There's sharp pain in her nose but Rose doesn't touch it. She lets the bottle fall to the floor where it lands on its side, the clear liquid dripping out, pooling to leave a stain that will last longer than either of them.

Chapter 16

March 15th 1981

I scratch a line into the wall with the piece of brick that I'd previously worked free. I knocked it off with my spoon a couple of weeks ago, when I still had a spoon to use. I don't have any utensils now. They still bring me my meals, but they don't bother with the knives and forks. It is as though they know the food will come back, so why bother getting them out in the first place? I began my hunger strike on 8th March, exactly one week ago. After the first few days I had headaches so terrible that I could hardly see. Then as I made sure to drink the six pints of salted water each day as I'd been instructed to, it was as if my body adjusted. Now, heading into the second week, I can feel a change again. My physical self has not altered much. I've been warned that my body will start to eat itself, sourcing goodness and fat from wherever it can. I can walk steadily, I can see no loss of my leg muscles and once those damn headaches passed my vision was as good as it ever was. Strangely, I don't even feel hungry anymore.

I've had no visits from my wife in three weeks despite the visiting orders I sent and my plea to Mary for her to get Bronwyn back in. I trust Mary, a fact which surprises me in itself, after all, I shot her son, but we had a deal and I know how much she wants Rose gone so I know she'll bring Bronwyn in to me.

Rose.

I have made arrangements for her. It was difficult, because it is a personal situation – not work related – but not impossible. If you look hard enough and use the right names you will always find someone to do your bidding. Soon Rose will be out of Mary's life. And for Mary's sake, Bronwyn had better be back in mine.

There is no sense in getting impatient; I have nothing else to do but wait.

During our waiting periods we talk a lot; myself and the other men, the ones that I think of as my brothers, are within hearing distance. We have started to 'tell books', and these are my best times. We have no actual books except the bible, and instead of making up stories we tell each other novels that we recall from memory. I can get lost in these times. We are writing letters too, smuggling them out and sending them to anybody who might listen; media, newspapers, television stations, politicians – anybody who we can think of who might spread the word on what we are doing here. We have a radio, an old wind up one and we listen to the news as much as we can. All of our contraband is smuggled in to us and collectively our favourite visitors are Brenda the Mule and Kimberley 'tits' Magee. Brenda is renown around Newry for the amount of stuff she is capable of hiding inside her, and 'Tit's' Magee, as her name suggests, has tits so massive that she can hold bulky items underneath them. They are good girls, humorous and loyal. Unlike my wife, I think darkly whenever she crosses my mind.

I digress. Our radio is vital, so that we know exactly what is happening outside and it gladdens our hearts when we hear of marches and demonstrations on our behalf. I think about Bronwyn, I wonder if she is marching. I think not, I think she is sitting at home, mourning this 'Emma' and regretting grassing me up. Wasting her life.

I can hear some of my mates getting ready to meet their visitors. I take a long drink of my salt water, swish it around my mouth, trying to get rid of the bad smell of bacteria trying to breed on the nothingness inside me.

Although I've not had word of a visitor it might be today. I live in hope.

Chapter 17

March 15th 1981

It's the first day in the three weeks of her new job that she doesn't jog straight home. Instead, she is meeting Alia in the town, in the café on the main street. Alia is there when she arrives, hot chocolate and cakes already ordered and on the table.

"I was going to bus home, but I'll have to run after all this!" says Bronwyn as she slides into the chair opposite her mother.

"Nonsense, you're too thin," says Alia, but softens her words with a smile. "You look happier though."

Bronwyn tosses her hair. She knows she looks good; she *feels* good. In part it is the running; she's done it every day, to and from work, even when a light covering of snow came down in the last week of February. Work has helped too, just the notion of having something to get up for, somewhere she needs to be at a certain time. She sees the same people, new people, and after a week of passing parents bringing their children through the gates in the morning it became only natural to exchange pleasantries and then, longer conversations. And from these new, almost-friendships, has come more work in the form of Bronwyn getting her mending and alteration service back up and running. The mothers that she talks with have to work themselves, nobody is flush in this age, and they don't have time to sew their kid's clothes. None of them have harassed her about being a 'supergrass', maybe they don't know, or maybe what she can offer them is more important than banding together in the name of the men. Bronwyn offers a cheap rate, and the mother's hand her whatever they need doing. She goes home, spends the afternoon working, relishing the ache as she bends over the sewing machine, taking them back the next day and handing over clothes for cash. She hasn't had any alcohol in three weeks, and most evenings she is so tired from working that she doesn't even want any.

She's never spoken to so many people, and she mentions this to Alia now as they sip at their hot drinks.

"You always had loads of friends, more than I could keep track of," replies Alia. "But at some point, I looked round and realised it was just Rose and Dan who were left."

At her best friend's name Bronwyn feels a pang of guilt. She hasn't seen or spoken to Rose since the morning of the job interview. She's stepped away from them all, deliberately, she realises now. Because there is only so much you can do to try and help people before you have to force them to stand on their own two feet. She hasn't seen Danny either, but she knows that he is now on the hunger strike. He is another matter. Rose, she lets herself think of her, but thoughts of Dan are too much, too painful.

"Maybe I should see Rose," she muses, half speaking to herself. "Hopefully she's settled in and she's getting along better."

Alia looks like she doesn't approve. She reaches across the table, takes Bronwyn's hand in her own and squeezes it. "Just remember, you come first, okay?"

"Do you want to walk over there with me?" asks Bronwyn, suddenly.

"What, now?"

"Yeah, why not?" it seems like a perfect idea, if Alia is there it will be someone to help the conversation along, especially if Mary and Connor are there, too. And with her mother's presence, she can leave when she wants on the pretext of having to get Alia back home.

As Alia agrees and they finish their drinks, Bronwyn is struck by a thought. *I never used to have to prepare myself so much to see Rose. What happened to us?*

Alia looks uncomfortable as they walk into the Dean's territory. Bronwyn tells her not to worry, that Connor and Mary are people, just like them. And as they walk up Mary's front path, she sees her mother looking almost longingly at the house.

"It's a decent area," Alia says, grudgingly.

Bronwyn knocks on the door, but they are startled by footsteps approaching them from behind. It's Mary, looking cross, as seems the norm to Bronwyn.

"She's not in," Mary declares as she moves in between them and puts her key in the lock. "The girl finally went back to work."

"Oh," says Bronwyn. "Well, that's good, if things are getting back to normal."

Mary fixes her with such a stare that Bronwyn widens her eyes.

"I wanted to speak to you, though," says Mary and then stops, looks over at Alia.

"This is my mother, Alia," Bronwyn says by way of introduction.

Alia nods, attempts a smile, but Mary simply turns back to Bronwyn. "I'd like a word, come in for a second, won't you?"

Bronwyn looks helplessly at Alia, who shrugs in reply. Mary opens the door, holds it open for Bronwyn, and then closes the door just as it looks like Alia might slip through.

"Hey!" exclaims Bronwyn.

"This won't take long," Mary snaps as she unwinds her scarf and hangs it on the banister. "Have you visited your husband lately?"

"No, why?" Bronwyn, annoyed at Mary rudely shutting her mother out, puts one hand on her hip and glares at Mary. "Why do you care so much about him anyway?"

"I don't care!" Mary raises her voice, seems to realise she is shouting and takes a deep breath. "I hear things, I know what's happening in there and I know… I don't want you to have any regrets, that's all."

"What would I have to regret?" Bronwyn is genuinely nonplussed. "He's not dying, it's not like he's going anywhere."

"Oh, Bronwyn," Mary's voice is quiet now and she almost looks sad. "But he is, they all are."

It doesn't occur to Bronwyn to ask how Mary hears things, being on the 'other side' she should hear nothing, and anything she does hear in the way she is suggesting should surely be celebrated.

Bronwyn doesn't want to hear anymore; the one good thing about Alia is that she doesn't try and talk to her about Dan, unlike Mary. It seems to be the only thing on her mind whenever Bronwyn sees her. She stands up straight, and says, firmly, "I have to go now, tell Rose I'll try and see her soon." Bronwyn fumbles behind her for the catch, pulls the door open and stumbles out straight into Alia. "Come on, Mum, we're going."

Alia hurries after her, struggles to match Bronwyn's gait. Behind them, they hear Mary's door slam loudly.

Chapter 18

March 15th 1981

Despite what Mary thinks, Rose hasn't been going to work. She went in the office, once, a few weeks ago and told her manager that she couldn't come back yet, that Connor needed her, yes, her boyfriend, he'd been shot, and she would do her best to return to work the following Monday morning.

She had been hoping for some sympathy, a little bit of kindness but it turned out that the manager, Frank O'Hara, knew all about the situation. There was no kindness to be found here, and as she stood in the open plan office while the workforce tried to pretend they were not listening, she realised that like her mother's house and Mary's home, this was another place where she was no longer welcome.

"Maybe it's for the best, at the moment." The words could have easily been spoken with sympathetic undertones but they weren't. They were hard and punchy, like O'Hara's glare.

And as she had walked out, probably for the last time, she realised what a lonely place it was when you were ostracised by everyone.

There was a girl at work, Marie McLoughlin, who Rose always sat next to. She had chosen Marie – actually they had chosen each other – as they were both quiet and reserved. It never quite escalated into a friendship, but it was the closest thing Rose had had to one in the workplace. As she had walked out after speaking to Mr O'Hara, she had seen Marie at her desk. Rose had paused, desperate that someone at least smile at her or exchange a few words. Marie had watched her walk all the way down the bank of desks and when Rose had stopped, Marie's wide-eyed, innocent expression had changed into that of a rabbit caught in the headlights.

"Marie...," Rose heard how dejected her own voice sounded, and cringed.

Marie looked away, sharply, her eyes now big and scared. Marie snatched up the telephone, hooked her finger and began to dial a number.

Rose had breathed in, jaggedly. She knew her face was red and sweat patches had formed under her arms.

"I'm sorry," she whispered, and half ran out of the office.

She hasn't told Mary that she can't go to work anymore. Mary doesn't speak to her anymore anyway, not since the incident with the bleach.

After the bottle had hit her face she had escaped upstairs to the bathroom, watching as her nose swelled and prodding at the tiny cut on the bridge. She had bathed it in cold water and sat in her room until Connor returned. It took a good ten minutes for her to summon the courage to go downstairs. She heard them in the kitchen, Mary and Connor, talking in hushed voices.

This is it, she had thought, *show time*. This is where Connor would realise exactly how his mother had treated his girlfriend, and the thought of Connor taking her hand, showing their unity and announcing that they were moving out was what spurred her on.

She stood in the doorway of the kitchen. They were at the table, silent now, Mary staring off into the distance, Connor shaking his head, drumming his fingers on the table. They both looked up as she loitered, Connor being the first to move. He came around the table, still limping but not relying on his crutches so much anymore. She'd folded into herself as he approached, preparing to fall into the welcome circle of his open arms. He'd pulled up short of her, just out of reach of touching distance.

"Ma told me what you did," he had said as he scrutinised her face. "Jesus, Rose, it's..." He had stopped, sighed heavily. "Just be more careful, okay?"

She had blinked, swivelled to look in disbelief at Mary. Mary, still seated, folded her arms and didn't even balk at Rose's stare.

"Dinner is nearly ready," Mary said after long seconds of silence, still looking directly at Rose.

"Good, I'm starving," replied Connor and made his way back to the table.

He pulled out a chair for Rose, so she had no choice but to join them. All through the meal and every day afterwards she wondered what lie Mary had told Connor. Neither of them ever told her. She hadn't found out what she was supposed to have done to herself.

It was the day after that she had gone to the office, and since then she had spent every day in her old childhood hiding spot at the library. She took a table in the far corner, around the back of the medical journal section, and she was rarely disturbed there. Even the librarians didn't look up anymore when she came in each morning. She is like a ghost. She is invisible.

Today she sits like every other day. She pulls out a couple of journals and opens them to random pages. She places a notebook and pen on the desktop and then closes her eyes. Every day she thinks about her mother, the man who is her birth father, Mary and Connor and Bronwyn and Danny. It doesn't escape her that she spends all day thinking about all these people who don't even talk to her or give her a second thought anymore.

The magic that she had with Connor is vanishing. Gone are the days when they would walk down dark alleyways and without warning he would stop, push her against a wall and drag the clothes off her lower body. She thinks of those times a lot and the instances where he wouldn't even remove her clothes, just pull her skirt up and push her underwear aside. She had glowed for days after each such occurrence, and it hits her that they haven't been together like that since the morning that Mary found her in Connor's bed.

Most days, sitting in the library, the thoughts get too much. An actual headache brews, starting at her temples and moving down through her neck and shoulders, just like it is now. She gets a paperclip out of her coat pocket and pushes her sleeve up. With uniform precision, she scratches at the underside of her wrist, until the blood starts to bubble up and leaks out, along with the hurt.

Chapter 19

March 22nd 1981

Two weeks in and I've lost the taste for cigarettes. This devastates me, as smoking was something to do, or rather, a way to take a break, even from doing nothing. A roll-up is a way to break up the monotony of the day, a way to break up the twenty-four hours. I've smoked since I was a teenager, not so much out of the enjoyment of it, but everyone else was and then, like almost everyone else, because I needed it. I still think I need it, but my body won't accept it. My senses are so heightened right now that even sparking up sends me into a spin of nausea. One of the screws wears a ghastly aftershave, even before the strike the scent of it would make me gag but now it's ten times worse. I can smell him coming long before I hear him, and I cover my face with whatever is within reach. Still the smell permeates, invading my nostrils until my eyes water.

Today was the first day that I've vomited back up the water I've been drinking. It's a bad sign, really bad, but one that I was told to expect. When I threw up the water it seemed to generate a tick in my left eye. Hours later and it still hasn't stopped, no matter how much I brush at it or pinch the surrounding skin.

There's something going on out in the hall. It sounds like a beating and using the wall I pull myself up slowly. Everything I do is slow now, moving at a snail's pace. Up until a few days ago I willed my body to move quicker, but it became obvious it wouldn't and all I was doing in trying was using precious energy that I should be conserving.

"Seany," I call to my neighbour, wincing at my voice, which sounds like a bleat.

"Danny, boy." Sean's voice booms out in response. "How are you doing, lad?"

Sean is not on the hunger strike yet, we have got all the shortlisted men on it and the others will now only commence striking when somebody dies.

I list my symptoms to him, not seeking compassion, but we are frank in here. You don't try and hide things because someone might have a tip or a trick that could help.

"Did you take in more water after you were sick?" Sean asks now.

"Yeah, I've kept it down so far," I reply.

His response is soothing, assuring, then we move on, discussing any news that anyone has heard from the outside world today. He is telling me about the men who are in the hospital wing, updating me on their individual situations, when I see someone walking down the corridor. It's Bronwyn, and my fragile heart leaps in my chest as I tune out Sean and grip the bars to watch her. She's looking good, really smart and really fucking together. Here is the Bronwyn that I knew all those years ago and I'm reminded of how I felt when I stood shakily in front of the priest on our wedding day. I'd thought I might fall down and even the nip of whiskey I'd taken had done nothing for my nerves. Then she'd come down the aisle, walking next to her mother, who she claimed had been both mother and father to her, defying tradition with her head held high as only she could. As soon as I clapped eyes on her in her simple wedding gown my fright dissipated. It was just Bron, there was nothing to be nervous about. It would have been weird if we hadn't got married, we were that good of a fit.

Vaguely I can hear Sean repeating my name, his voice getting a little louder with each call. I shush him. I want to watch her walking to me. She hasn't seen me yet and I become the voyeur, feeling little flips and twists in a place that hasn't been hard in weeks. I can stand it no more and I put my arm through the window as far as it will go.

"Bron!" I shout, and the strength of my voice startles me.

As soon as I call out, a mist comes over the corridor, like the one that hangs over the Clanrye River where I used to fish. I flap my hand uselessly, waiting for the fog to clear. When it does I realise what happened. The mist wasn't in the hallway, it was a film that slipped over my own eyes and Bronwyn, she was never out there at all.

My body sags, my arms slipping back inside the cell. As I fall down, I clutch sightlessly at anything solid. I find no purchase and succeed only in scratching my overgrown fingernails down the door as I slide ever downwards. Sean's voice, calling my name over and over, rings in my ears as I land in a heap on the floor.

Chapter 20

March 22nd 1981

There is someone at Billy's grave when Mary strolls through the gates. She clutches at her handbag, works the handles with anxious fingers. There is never anybody at Billy's grave, and Mary has been coming here a lot in the last couple of weeks, more in the last ten days than she's visited in the last two decades. Each day she comes it gets a little easier, and memories of happy times that she has not allowed herself to think of are coming back, still with sharp stabs of pain, but the hurt has been dulled a little. It has been a revelation, and it is ironic that she's only found out because of the girl who pushed her out of her home.

But this person, this woman, Mary can see now, kneeling on Billy. Who is she? Not a sister, for he only had brothers. Mary pauses at a plot a few rows back and places her hand on the steel fence that borders the gravesite. She's not young, this stranger, in fact Mary would put her at around her own age. And she's got flowers, the damn cheek of it! Mary grips at her own small bouquet; handpicked daffs from her own garden, and looks at the other woman's offering, great big daisy gerberas, not in season, far too fancy and not at all suitable for a grave.

The woman rises, quickly, and turning sharply she strides off towards the side of the church. Mary looks quickly down at the grave she is standing beside. The Parks family is buried here, the dates register as Mary concentrates on not looking at the departing woman. Margret died over a hundred years ago, but it's a family plot, there's also a son-in-law, John, and a son, Samuel. She thinks of what her own plot will be like, with Connor eventually sleeping beside her. Her face darkens as she imagines Rose being tossed in alongside them and she tightens her fingers around the rusty metal fencing of the plot.

Thoughts of the girl have raised her already heightened temper and she stalks down to Billy's grave, sinking to her knees on the grass. She picks up the bouquet of daisy's and holding it between thumb and forefinger she puts them to once side. She takes the band off her daffodils and one by one pokes them into the memorial vase. The motion soothes her, and when she's done she picks up the gerberas again. She thinks about going back to the little outhouse adjoining the church and getting another vase to put these in. Maybe she wasn't a former lover of Billy, perhaps she was a sister-in-law or an old childhood friend. Mary breathes deeply, calmly. She's always calmer when she's here, Billy's plot has been her saving grace these last few weeks. The sun pierces the grey clouds and the warmth that comes with it envelopes her as she unwraps the cellophane. The woman left the price on, Mary notes, how tacky. And as she pulls out the flowers and crumples up the wrapping, a small card topples onto the grass. Picking it up she see it's an envelope, a tiny one, and as Mary sees her own name written on it she almost drops it again. She turns around, left and right, and sees nobody in sight at all. She is the only person in the graveyard. Slipping a finger underneath the flap, she opens the envelope and takes out the little card. Five words are written on it, and it is unsigned.

Mary, come to the church.

She inhales deeply, thinks back to the woman with the gerberas. She didn't look threatening; her coat had been fitted, buckled tightly at her waist, unlikely to have been concealing anything. Guns, it's always guns that Mary thinks about, ever since Billy, always wondering if now, some twenty years later, his people are going to come looking for her, making her pay for his loss of life. A hopeful thought comes to her; generations have passed and the woman is a descendent of Billy. His brothers want to know her, want to get to know their nephew. It is unlikely, she admits that much to herself, the troubles are even more ferocious now than they were back then. Simultaneously she despises herself for still hoping. Regardless of what it is about, Mary wants to know what this woman wants, and so she stands, straightens her coat, stuffs the cellophane into her pocket and walks towards the church.

Inside it's cold and rather stark. Twenty-four pews in two rows, the only redeeming feature in Mary's opinion is the beautiful blue stained-glass window at the far end. Saint Mary's has been renovated since she came here for Billy's funeral. The decoration has not changed Mary's feelings. It's still cold and unforgiving. Father Pettit has gone now, of course, as has his successor, Father Rooney. This house belongs to the Archdeacon Liam Boyle these days, though right now it seems he is not at home. The stranger with the gerberas is though, sitting in the front pew, head bent as if in prayer. Mary walks up the aisle, heels clicking against the floor announcing her arrival.

"Hello, Mary," says the woman softly and stands up. "I have an instruction for you from your friend, Danny."

She is thrown, of all the reasons the woman wanted to see her not once had Danny Granger crossed her mind as being one of them.

"This won't take long," says the woman, her tone brisk now, though still soft and quiet. "Wednesday the 1st April you will need to take your son out for the evening. Give it a good couple of hours, come back to the house after 9 p.m and your problem will be solved."

The woman offers Mary a smile and makes to leave.

"Wait!" Mary catches her sleeve. The woman's smile disappears and she shakes her arm free of Mary's grasp. "My problem, you mean... do you mean the girl?"

The woman nods, once, solemnly. "She'll be gone by the time you get home. Okay?"

Mary wants to shout, *no, it's not okay*, but even though she has so many questions, she can't think of a single one to ask.

Another smile, another nod, and the woman squeezes past Mary in the pew and walks back to the doors. Mary turns around when she can no longer hear her. The stranger has gone, and Mary doesn't even know her name.

She sinks onto the hardwood pew, bows her head, unsure how she should be feeling. Emotions are pushing at her and she plucks one out and holds onto it.

I'm relieved, she thinks. *It'll be over, very soon, and I'll have Connor back with me, just me and him, how it should be.*

Chapter 21

March 25th 1981

As they stand on the roadside Bronwyn reaches for Alia's hand. Her mother looks down at her daughter's touch and squeezes her hand. They exchange a glance before both looking back at the building that looms before them.

"I'll come in with you, if you like," offers Alia.

Bronwyn shakes her head. "No, I need to do this alone." She darts a look at Alia. "You'll wait for me though, right?"

"Of course I will, I'll be right here when you come out."

The prison is spread out, surrounded by tall concrete fences topped with curved barbed wire. A watch tower looms up, floodlights dotted throughout the grounds. There's no escaping here, that much is apparent. *And my husband is inside.* It's a grim thought in an even grimmer place.

The guard looks her up and down as she checks in. She can feel his eyes and she wonders what he's looking at. It's still freezing; she's padded out in thick jeans, boots and a puffer jacket over her jumper. She meets his stare, forces him to look away first.

She's transferred to a different guard inside and this one merely gives her a disdainful look as he instructs her to follow him.

"Granger is in the hospital wing," he says as he walks.

"What? Why?" This is news to Bronwyn.

He slows and looks sidelong at her. "He collapsed two days ago."

I should know this, she thinks, angrily. *No matter what's happening between us I'm still his next of kin. Why has nobody told me this?*

"Why wasn't I told?" she asks.

The guard shrugs and looks momentarily perplexed. "Do you have a telephone?"

She shakes her head.

"There's probably a letter on the way to you, then."

"Is he... is it bad?" Her voice is tentative now and she wonders what awaits her.

The guard smiles, showing an overcrowded mouth of teeth, and she stares at them, full of dislike for him.

"See for yourself," he says, and pushes open a door, stepping back to allow her through.

She ducks under his arm, throws him a hateful look. The door swings back and closes. Through the porthole window she can see him, still smiling.

She turns her back on him.

She is in a room, a single cell that holds a single bed. She half turns, raises her hand to knock at the door, opens her mouth to call for the guard.

All of his bluster and he's shown me into the wrong fucking room. She raps on the door, once, and then she hears him call her name.

"Bron."

The breath that she had drawn in comes whooshing back out in a gasp as she looks over her shoulder. Her hand, poised to knock, comes to her face and she bites down on her knuckles.

"Come on over," he says and lifts his head a little. "It is you, isn't it?"

She's beside his bed in seconds, standing over him, looking down at the wasted body and the thin legs. Her gaze moves up the bed, landing on his eyes. They are huge, protruding from his gaunt face. His right arm is up, moving to and fro. She knows she should take his hand, but it's all wrong, it can't be his hand, the hand that has grabbed her hair roughly when he's in a foul temper, smacked her once around the face in anger, stroked her cheek, cupped the small of her back as they walk.

She breathes his name, settles for touching the tips of her fingers against his.

He smiles.

"I was worried it wasn't really you," he rasps. "I've been having some funny moments, when I think I see you, but you're not really there, I was worried I was having an episode."

She doesn't know what to say. He hasn't ever confessed to worrying about anything before, not in all the years she's known him. And never has Bronwyn been lost for words, usually it's the opposite problem, she's full of them, too many of them.

"Is it worth it?" she rakes her eyes up and down his body again.

"Ah, I'm all right," he replies, struggling into a sitting position as though to prove his state of health. "You'll not get rid of me yet."

Sitting up he looks better, not like the old Danny, she can't imagine him ever looking that way again, but he doesn't look so close to death this way.

"Do you want a blanket?" she asks, helplessly.

He shakes his head. "No, they rub too much, they irritate me. I'll have a sheet put over me later."

It hits her then, right at that moment, when they are having a normal conversation like a normal couple. He's going all the way with this, he's not going to stop and pull himself back from the brink, not even for her. She almost laughs at that thought. Why would he do it for her? She's the one who put him in here, if she hadn't called the police he would be back at home and she'd be serving him up a breakfast right about now. Sadness and hate burn side by side and she moves away from the bed a little bit.

Should I take responsibility for calling the police? Should I apologise to him? If I did would I mean it?

"Bron," he calls and she sees that he's squinting at her. "Don't move so far away, please, my eyes..."

I've done this, if he wasn't in here he wouldn't be on a hunger strike... The thoughts tumble over themselves, each one coming to her like a punch in her gut.

"Oh my GOD!" it's more than a scream, it's a primitive sound that she's never heard before, especially coming from herself. It is raw. It is animal.

She wrenches the door open, pushes past the guard and sprints down the corridor and out of The Maze.

*

Alia has opted to stay out of the prison grounds and while she waits for Bronwyn she walks slowly up and down. Stopping occasionally she looks at the prison. She finds it heartbreakingly easy to believe that Dan is inside. He was always headed that way, no matter how much she tried to bring him up and care for him and feed him. Like Rose, there was always going to be a climax. She's not sure who she feels for more, Rose or Danny.

Both of them have been led by others, Rose with her boyfriend, Danny with the I.R.A. Is it a coincidence that they both had parents who were either not there or totally useless? Yet they had both had her, Alia, and she'd taken them both in and raised them alongside her own daughter. She had scolded them and even raised a hand to Dan once, when he was caught shoplifting. In her eyes she never treated them any different to her own natural born, and just look at them now. She can see Bronwyn running now, she can hear her too, sucking in great gulps of air as she sprints, head down towards Alia. She's moving so fast that Alia has to shoot her arms out to stop her running straight past her. They spin in the road, clutching at each other as Alia tries to centre her daughter.

"He's not fecking dead, is he?" Alia shouts as she can think of no other reason for Bronwyn's hysterics.

Bronwyn shakes her head, tears flying off her cheeks. Alia leaves one hand on Bronwyn's shoulder and with the other she pats her palm gently over Bronwyn's face.

"He's going to die, though," Bronwyn sobs. "I can't believe he's doing this."

Alia draws her daughter close, and latched together they begin to walk. She doesn't know what to say, the usual 'it'll be all right' really does not apply here. It won't be okay, not unless Thatcher and her Brits back down and give these men what they want. And it's not much that they want, really, the right to be seen as political prisoners, to wear their own clothes, to have parcels and letters and visitors.

As they pass the main entrance Alia looks up at the watch tower. Tears spring to her own eyes, unchecked, as a sudden image of Danny comes to her, aged twelve, at high school. He'd broken his arm on the football field and the school had called Alia. Not his foster parents at the time or social services, but her. She had taken him to the hospital to get it set and clutched at his good arm while he cried silent tears. He's like a son, he was always like a son, albeit one she didn't like at times, and now he's going to die.

"Shall we go home?" Alia asks, once Bronwyn has quietened down.

Bronwyn shrugs in reply and, still holding hands, they walk to the bus stop.

Chapter 22

April 1st 1981

Mary thinks constantly about getting Connor out of the house on the date she has been given. It shouldn't be as difficult as she's finding it, and she sees all too clearly now how little time she spends with Connor away from home, with just the two of them. Because home is where they both want to be. But she's got to get him out so whoever is doing Danny's bidding can get Rose to move out. The pub isn't an option; if Connor wants to go there he goes with his workmates. Dinner is too formal, Rose would be expected to attend.

In the days after her meeting with the stranger in the church, Mary goes back and forth, clutching at any options she can think of. After a while it makes her feel sick, that she can't think of someplace to take her own boy, just the two of them.

But it's because we like to be at home, together, just the two of us, she constantly reassures herself.

And on the first day of April, the day that Rose will be out of their lives, Mary awakes to an epiphany.

It's so glaringly obvious that she can't believe she didn't think of it before. She sits bolt upright in bed and leans over to switch the lamp on. Peering at the clock she sees it is only just past 5 a.m. Wrapping her housecoat around her she creeps along the landing to Connor's room.

He's just stirring, rubbing his eyes as she walks in and she's glad the witch isn't in his bed.

"Ma," he whispers. "What are you doing up?"

"I need you to meet me after work, just you, outside Saint Mary's," she replies, softly. "Will you?"

"Saint Mary's, what for?" he looks perplexed.

"I'll tell you when we're there, it's… it's to do with your Dad."

She waits, holding her breath, mentally crossing herself for using Billy that way. Eventually Connor nods his agreement.

"Just us though, okay?" she clarifies. "It's a personal matter. It's a family thing."

"Okay, okay, I'll be there."

She withdraws from the room, hurries back to her own bedroom and sinks back into her still warm bed. So rarely do they discuss Billy Dean that she is confident Connor will be at the church. She will show him his father's grave, she's never taken him there before. She just has to make sure and keep him there.

Though the sun hasn't even risen yet she throws off the covers. Today is a game changer and there is no more chance of sleep for Mary.

Chapter 23

April 1st 1981

Bronwyn dimly registers that she has been drunk for a week. Not falling down, throwing up, all out pissed, but she has drank every single day since she visited Danny. After Alia and her got off the bus and said their goodbyes, Bronwyn headed straight for the off-licence. It wasn't even open but she didn't care what passers-by thought of her standing outside, kicking her heels. All that she knew was she had to deaden the thoughts and the memory.

When the proprietor unlocked the door Bronwyn almost fell into the shop. Eyes raw from crying, Bronwyn had no particular medicinal fluid in mind. Anything, any product would do.

When she got home with her selection she didn't even inspect it, rather, she pulled the tab on the nearest item – a can of Harp – and took it down to sit by Emma where she remained for the rest of the day.

The following day, and each of the others after that, she went to work. She still jogged, though it was much more difficult, and she still took in the clothes that needed mending from the other mothers. Once back at home she rushed through the sewing, knowing that her stitching wasn't as neat as usual, but consoling herself that her customer's wouldn't mind. As long as they don't have to do it themselves, she thought, wryly.

Now a whole week has passed. No correspondence has been received from Long Kesh – not even the original letter – and she has heard nothing further about Danny or his condition. In equal measure she wants to telephone them and also to forget about it, about him, and ignore his imminent death.

She sits beside Emma, using her sewing scissors to tidy up the patchy grass around the tiny memorial.

"I know exactly how you were created," she whispers with a smile.

How many people can say that? Though it's easier to pinpoint exact moments of passion when you have been with someone as long as she's been with Dan and the moments don't happen as frequently as they once did.

It was before Christmas, snow was on the ground and the covered over concrete had put Bronwyn in such a good mood she had pulled the kitchen curtain open all the way. Dusk had fallen but the white of the snow had cast an ethereal glow around the garden. It had been breathtakingly beautiful. Danny was home from work, he had still had his job then, and he had come up soundlessly behind her in the kitchen and wrapped his arms around her waist. It was an unexpected, tender moment, one that had brought tears to her eyes, for the only reason that she couldn't remember the last time he had touched her like that. They had stood looking out at the garden for ages, until she had twisted in his arms to face him.

"Let's go outside," she whispered, tilting her face up to look at his. "Like when we were kids."

His lips had twitched in a smile. She remembers it all; how his hands had squeezed the small of her back, how his eyes had turned so dark they were almost liquid coal. Like the children they once were, they ran hand in hand outside and picked their way through the snow down to the train tracks. A snowball fight had evolved into physical tussling, and when their stomachs hurt from laughing they had sunk into the snow together. She recalls now that they did not feel the cold, and how afterwards she had looked at his face, red cheeked and hope and happiness had risen within her.

The hope soon faded, in fact it melted away with the snow, and when normal life resumed they were back to their old selves.

"We had some good times though, Emma," Bronwyn whispered to the not-quite-carcass of their child.

And as she sinks the last can of Harp she stares out over the fields. There's nothing now; no Danny, no Emma and no snow.

Chapter 24

April 1st 1981

When Rose wakes she rolls over in the bed and stares at the wall. It's April, winter is turning into spring.

And though the seasons have changed, Rose thinks, *nothing in my life has changed at all. If anything it's only got worse.*

She can't even get up today and pretend to go to work. Perhaps if she stays here, deep in the warmth and relative safety of the bed and the room that nobody comes into, they won't even notice that she's not left the house. It's an intriguing thought, a test, really, to see how invisible she has really become. Connor's not happy, Mary's not happy, and Rose has run out of ideas to try and make up for the disappointment she is to them.

It's still dark outside as she makes her way through the hallway to the bathroom. She uses the toilet as quietly as possible and as she darts back to the spare room she hears Connor's alarm go off. She pauses in the hallway, near his door, thinks about going in, just to get a smile or... anything really, anything except the horrible, flat, polite atmosphere that exists between them.

She is weary though, and through her open door she can see the dark cave of her bed. Forgoing Connor she slips back into the spare room and pulls the duvet over her head.

*

Later, much, much later when she wakes again, the house in still in darkness and she pulls the clock around to face her, squints at it. It's almost 6pm and she has slept for another twelve hours solid. The realisation of this should shock her, but she feels nothing.

After a while she becomes aware of a rustling noise. Someone is out on the landing. It could be Mary or it could be Connor. Do they not wonder where she is? Do they not think to check this room? For if they are both home they know that she will be too, at this time of day.

She waits for the tears or the stomach-churning hurt, but nothing comes. *And I feel flat, flat and dark and like a waste of a body. I've fallen down to the very deepest, darkest depths of rock bottom. And I'm not going to crawl out of here.*

The thoughts come thick and fast and she duly notes each one, without surprise, without fear. All emotions are gone. Even cutting her skin doesn't bring any feelings anymore.

Seconds, minutes or an hour have passed when the door to the spare room is pushed open. Again with no reaction, she regards the man standing in the doorway. He is wearing a balaclava, this detail she does note.

Just like the night they shot Connor, she thinks.

She can't see his face, but his eyes stare back at her.

And what now, what happens now?

The lack of interest that she has at the stranger standing in her doorway is almost interesting. *And I could laugh at that, if laughter were possible.*

He's by her bed, reaching out an arm and pulling her roughly to a sitting position. She doesn't struggle, she has no fight and no wish to fight. She realises that she is nodding to herself as she lets herself be led from the bed. Dimly she wonders where Mary and Connor are. Has this man already got them? Are they tied up, already shot, dead, even? *Are my senses so dulled that I didn't even hear gunshots?*

He halts her on the landing, just at the top of the stairs. He gesticulates upwards and she raises her face to the ceiling, an act which only serves to make her even wearier.

That was the rustling that she heard, the loft hatch opening, being pushed to one side, the rope that was tied to the beam of the interior roof, hanging down from the eaves and appearing through the opening, arranged just so to form a noose.

The air coming from the exposed roof is cold, she feels that much and she crosses her arms across her chest.

"It's time for you to go." The man speaks for the first time, his voice quiet.

She can feel his breath on her ear and she understands. This is where she begs, where she says that she'll do anything, she won't tell a soul if he'll just *let her go*. Just let her walk out of Mary's house and not come back.

She nods again, more to herself than *him*. It makes sense, everything clicks into place.

"Okay," she says, still nodding. "Okay, then."

Chapter 25

April 1st 1981

The church is a peaceful place where Mary can sit undisturbed. It's cold, terribly cold, like all places of worship seem to be, but she had anticipated this and the extra layers help, as does the flask of tea that she has bought along.

There is a fair bit of traffic here today, there are no services, but people are coming and going. The florist came before midday and arranged fresh flowers at the font, the cleaners arrived, vacuumed around her and left in the early afternoon. Worshipers came too, to pray, to cry soundlessly and some of them just to sit, like herself.

She went out to see Billy a few times, when she looked through the blue stained glass window and saw the sun's rays trying to peep out of the heavy white clouds. And then as it began to get dark, Connor arrived.

She led him to Billy's grave, handed him the flowers that she had picked for him to place there. He did so awkwardly, with what seemed like a degree of embarrassment. She was upset, she had envisaged this moment as an emotional connection between the three of them.

"Doesn't it make you feel sad?" she asks with disbelief.

He shrugs, fuelling her temper with his attitude.

"I didn't know him, I can't miss him, Ma," he protests. "I understand that you do because you were with him, you loved him. But I never knew him."

Mary turns away and traces her fingers over Billy's name. Connor is right, of course, but he should care, he *should* be upset. And, she has to stall him, she has to keep him here so Danny's men can invoke the forced removal of Rose from Mary's home.

"I suppose I'd like to talk about him sometimes," she says, still stroking at the grave. "And also, if you're serious about this girl, we need to talk. You need to be prepared about what your life will be like."

"Well, I already know, don't I?" he points to his wounded leg.

He is being flippant. *Like a teenager*, she thinks, *pushing me, pressing my buttons.* "This is serious, Connor." Her tone is mild and it pleases her that she's able to keep control.

He sighs, openly, but when he doesn't make a move to leave she begins to talk then, and even though he occasionally tries to interrupt and even though the temperature has dropped to surely below zero, he stays.

"And are you ready for this?" she demands, finally. "For staying at home because no public place will welcome you as a couple? Or what, are you going to move away, over into England? How are you going to raise your children, you have to pick a religion because you can't have it all ways, can you?"

At this he holds up his hands. "Woah, come on, Ma. We've only been together a few months, who's talking about kids and houses?"

She closes her eyes, very tired all of a sudden as she gets it. He's not serious about Rose. He was, or he thought he was, when they were sneaking around at night and it was all exciting and fresh and new, but he's changed his mind. Now he sees for himself that she would be a useless wife and homemaker, and he's been clapping eyes on a make-up free face and wild hair each morning. He has changed his mind.

Obviously he doesn't know how to tell the girl that he has realised how close he has come to being trapped. Because next there would be a child, and then he'd never get away. *Poor sod*, she thinks to herself. *But it'll be over soon.*

"I thought I'd go and see her friend, Bronwyn, maybe get the two girls together again. They were as close as anything but they've drifted apart. It's no good for Rose," Connor says, as he levers himself off Billy's headstone that he had so disrespectfully been perched on.

And Bronwyn has a big house all to herself, if Connor can get the two girls talking then it would be natural for Rose to stay at her best friend's house. Pleasure froths up inside of Mary at all of the loose ends being tidily knotted. Everyone would be happy; Mary would have Connor back, Bronwyn would have company, and the girl would have a home. Because as much as she despises her, Mary wouldn't like to see Rose homeless. After all, she's not a monster.

It's a pious thought, but a pleasing one.

She waves him off as they part at the gates. He heads towards the night bus, she walks home.

The house is in darkness, she notes, as she walks up the front path. A good sign, but not unusual, for if the girl were still in the home she would be ensconced in the spare room anyway, lights out and sleeping, even though it's only 7 o'clock.

She opens the front door and slips inside, shrugging off her coat and hanging it in the usual place over the banister. She stops, sniffs. Over the furniture polish and the faint stale aroma of Mary's cigarettes there is a definite scent of excrement and she is transported back to The Maze, being led down the corridor to see Danny. The peace that she had walking home is replaced with anger. The girl has gone and as a last act of defiance she's left some cat shit somewhere, Mary imagines. Mixed in with her contempt is a grudging admiration; she didn't think the girl had it in her.

She begins her hunt in the kitchen, but the room is exactly how she left it earlier. The aroma is stronger in the hallway and by the light of the lamp in the porch she checks behind the umbrella stand. Slowly she becomes aware of a creaking noise, so low she missed it until moving to the bottom of the stairs. Here though, she can hear it clearly. There used to be an old conifer tree in the garden of this house and one winter, a branch was damaged, either by lightening or in the near hurricane force winds. For weeks after the storm the branch had creaked until it drove Mary mad and she had Connor cut it down.

It's coming from the top of the house, somewhere in the darkness, and as Mary climbs the stairs the air changes. It's even colder up here and she can hear the wind that has picked up outside. Has the mad girl opened the windows before she left? Or is that how Danny's man got in, through a window? Annoyed, she picks up her pace, eager to find the offending open window and close it, to gain some heat back from which she's been so careful to preserve over the winter. She pulls herself up the last stair, spins around the top handrail and God, up here, the *smell*... She hasn't put the light on yet, she knows every inch of this house blindfolded but she has to see, and she reaches an arm out towards the switch, brushing something, something that is the cause of the creaking.

With a yell she pulls back and clutches her hand to her chest as though it was injured. Fabric, skin, something solid yet yielding that is out of place, that shouldn't be on the landing and which brings with it an underlying smell of urine and sweat.

She punches the light and sees the loft hatch hanging open.

So that's where the cold air is coming from. She has a split second to process the thought and then there is a scream, guttural, with an unearthly quality. She dodges around out of reach of the spinning, swinging body that creaks above her, seeking the source of the screamer. As her back hits the wall and she slides down to land on the carpet, she realises that she is the one who is screaming.

Chapter 26

April 11th 1981

A whole month on the hunger strike. There's a strange sense of pride that was only apparent once I began to adjust and feel..., not better, but like I still had some more mileage in me. I don't know why it happened, that day a couple of weeks ago when Bronwyn came I felt like I was close to death. Personally I think the fact that she ran out crying has spurred me on, as though I can't let that be the last contact we had with each other. Seany told me some of the other hunger strikers had recommended walking around as much as possible, just to stop the muscles dying in their legs and bodies. So I did and I continued with my salt water diet and so far I've not been sick anymore.

I'm still squinting though, my eyesight has always been pretty perfect, but the daylight through the window really hurts my eyes. Like a painting or a photo that spends years in direct sunlight my eyes are fading, just like the picture would.

I've had no visitors except a man a couple of days ago, I can't even think where he was from, it's a bit foggy, but he was talking about my power of attorney and how it will be shifted to Bron when it looks like I'm on my way out. This means she can instruct the prison doctors to intervene medically, shove tubes down my throat and force feed me if she so desires. I've made it clear that I don't want this, otherwise what is the point of the strikes? But the decision will be out of my hands. I need to see Bron again, I need to tell her that she mustn't do this. At the same time I consider it and her possible actions. If she does medically intervene then she obviously still cares. Or on the other hand, maybe not, maybe she's just not the sort of person who can have another man's death on her hands, perhaps she's not cut from the same cloth as Thatcher. Regardless, I want to see my wife. I want another chance to say the right thing to her, because I keep messing up and God knows, I've not got too many opportunities left.

The boys are doing okay, Bobby has gone downhill but he's still here. We are all still here and we're not budging. Today and yesterday we've had the crystal radio set on nonstop as we listen for results of the election. The results come in the early evening. It began as a low murmur, news passed to the men through windows, bars and pipes. Some occupants react differently; there was singing from one wing, shouts from another. Me and the half dozen others, we just sit and grin at each other. The screws come and tell us that Bobby had lost. Spitefully they await our reactions but we just keep on smiling. Confused, they slip away. They didn't know we have the radio and that we are aware of the news from the outside just as well as them. Now we reassure each other that Thatcher is not going to let this go too far. She can't afford to, the Brits are going to have to give in first, because now Bobby Sands is an officially elected Member of Parliament. They will have to give in to us now; they'll have to give us what we want. With this new hope we stand and we won't be broken. We will not meekly serve our time.

Chapter 27

April 14th 1981

Bronwyn has stopped going to bed at night because when she sleeps, she has to endure the horror of waking and she hates that first, bleary eyed moment of sanctuary before the events of the last few weeks crash down on her. With the help of coffee and some pills she swiped from Alia's bathroom cabinet, she's trying not to sleep at all.

It still hits her at inopportune moments of every day and night. Rose is gone. Dead. Hanged.

Hanged.

That's the part she just can't envisage, that she – anybody – would do that. An overdose, yes, like going into a forever sleep. But that, it's beyond any comprehension.

Then there's the thing that happened on the night of Rose's death. Again, it comes to her often, like a punch in the stomach or a slap around the face. It physically winds her, so whatever she is doing she has to stop while she doubles over, face flushed with shame.

*

Two weeks earlier:

When the snow melted away to patchy grey sludge Bronwyn decided that Emma's memorial stones needed cleaning. Carefully she gathered them and bought them into the house where she stood at the sink, washing and wiping them one by one. With each stone that she completed she allowed herself a mouthful of wine and the evening was passing almost pleasantly, and for the first time in ages she felt almost relaxed.

"Bronwyn?"

The sound of her name being called through the letterbox startled her and the last of Emma's pebbles slipped from her fingers, landing with a splash in the sink.

She swore, softly, wiping her hands, and made her way down the hall to the front door. Opening it, she found Connor on the step.

"Oh, hello," she smiled. Her heart did a funny little dance as she put her hand on her chest as if to stifle it. "Is Rose with you?"

He shook his head and she moved aside to let him in. She watched as he limped past her, down the hall and into the kitchen. Something snagged at her insides and she caught herself, forced her gaze away from him. There was danger here, tonight, she'd thought for some reason, which had been ridiculous. All he had said was her name. It was enough though. Her name, when he spoke it, wasn't innocent, it was deadly.

At the kitchen table they took the same seats that they had last time he was here. She poured them both a drink and as they regarded each other, almost warily, neither of them spoke.

She thought how to begin, to ask him if something was wrong, to enquire about Rose, who she hadn't seen since their dismal meeting of a couple of weeks ago. She calculated mentally and realised it was February when she last saw her best friend. The month of March had passed and in her lifetime she could never recall not seeing Rose for a whole calendar month before. Yet each time she had taken a breath to speak, her eyes landed on Connor's face and she forgot what she had intended to say. That face, it was exquisite, and his body being in such close proximity to her bought something inside her to the forefront which she could only describe as primal.

He must have seen it on her face, which was funny because she's normally so good at closing herself off, not letting anyone know what she's thinking. But he saw it, subconsciously she had opened herself to him, and she doesn't know who reached for whom first, but she flew from her chair and covered the short distance between them, ending up on his lap. His hands planted on her lower back, he broke away from her, his voice a low murmur.

"God, I wanted-"

She pressed her lips to his, not wanting him to talk because if he spoke the spell might be broken.

He seemed to understand, and there were no more attempts at talking. Not only speech was abandoned, but thoughts too. Bronwyn threw aside everything except feeling. That, she clung onto.

After she climbed off his lap, she adjusted her clothes and sat back in her chair. Her face was hot and fear pinpricked her. He hadn't pulled out, she hadn't given him the chance. He buttoned up his jeans, caught her watching him, and winked. She'd smiled cautiously, stood up, felt him sticky and damp on her thighs, and had drawn him into the living room. They had sat in front of the fire that wasn't switched on, settled into the sheepskin rug, close together, side by side, but not touching.

"Wish I'd have found you first," he said, without looking at her.

She had resented this; the accusation that she was somehow better than Rose. Or maybe she resented the mention of her friend.

"I'd have still been married," she replied, mildly.

"Imagine if you weren't."

That fact would have made no difference and she told him so. "You're a Prod," she said, knowing her words were hurtful and she backtracked a little. "Besides, it's always good at the beginning." It had been good with Dan, all those years ago.

"We should just enjoy the beginning then," he had said, reaching for her again.

The second time the sense of urgency had gone. She let him peel every item of clothing away from her and she made no move to cover herself. Her body had changed with all the running and for the first time in years she was almost proud of the way she looked. She took his clothes off too, scrutinised his form. He wasn't as tall as Danny or as muscled, but his body was lean, naturally skinny. She touched the dressing on his leg and registered how odd it was that she was with this man who had been so horribly injured at the hands of her husband. A chill came over the room and she got up to plug the fire in, leaving him on the rug, head propped up on one hand as he watched her.

Bang-bang-bang-BANG.

The thump of fists on the window broke her stride and she spun around, screamed at the sight of a face pressed up to the glass. In the darkness she saw a finger point to the front door and then the face withdrew.

She pulled on her jeans and braless, she wrapped her shirt around her. Connor dressed more slowly, only appearing at her shoulder as she opened the door to come face to face with a police officer.

Her first thought was of Danny and her breath shuddered through her as she thought of what she had been doing with Connor while her husband had been dying.

"You'll need to come with us," the Officer said, not even glancing at her exposed skin or her undone jeans. "There's been a fatality."

A second scream hovered near the surface until she realised that the policeman wasn't talking or even looking at her. He was speaking to Connor.

*

She's not seen him since that night. She's not surprised, fucking another woman while his girlfriend was committing suicide. She doesn't feel that she can face him either. Although at the funeral she will have to, as Alia keeps reminding her.

She confessed to her mother what they had done and the tears had spilt afresh at the thought that once she would have whispered a secret like that to Rose. Not *that* secret, obviously, but a similar man, had it been a different man. And the thing that made her cringe; Alia already knew. Apparently Officer Patsy McCreesh had enjoyed telling all of his colleagues and pals what he had witnessed between the Catholic mole who had shopped her husband and the Protestant man who had been the victim on the end of the husband's gun. *Perhaps that's what the original kneecapping was all about*, were the whispers going around Newry.

She's not been out since that night. Not to work or even jogging. Alia has been bringing her food, patiently cooking and then practically spoon feeding Bronwyn. She has been in hiding, but the funeral is now only days away and she has to go. Alia will flank her, but it's not the thought of the hatred from the community that she fears. It's seeing Connor again.

Chapter 28

April 14th 1981

I'm aware that I've got a visitor. They come as they please now I'm in the hospital. It's hard work to drag myself up to the surface and focus my eyes and when I finally manage it, I almost wish I had stayed asleep.

It's Mary Dean, perched on the edge of a chair by my bed. Her hands are curled into fists and she's clutching at my blanket. Her eyes are wild and even before she speaks I can tell that she's angry. Using my elbows, which are sore, I push myself half upright and wait for her to tell me why she's there.

"What did you do?" she hisses the words through clenched teeth.

I search my memory which is hazy and I recall my man, Kieran, who I'd sent to roust Rose out of the Dean's family home. I've not seen Kieran, I assume it went to plan though it was a long time ago, I think, but my hours blend into weeks here so I may be wrong. However, this is the only connection that Mrs Dean and I have had, apart from me shooting her son, that is.

"Are you talking about Rose James?"

"You stupid... *fuck*!"

She releases the bedding from her claw and grips my arm. I jerk away, study the indentations made in my skin by her nails. "What... I don't know what's happened."

She catches a hold of herself, looks over her shoulder before putting her face close to mine. "Your man killed the girl, he fecking well hung her."

I think I might be still asleep and dreaming, but then I look at the little half-moon marks she made on my arms and I know I'm not. How odd that Kieran would do that. I mean, I know the tricks that are used to frighten people into leaving and the threat of execution, by whatever means, is common, but to actually do it... I turn my head on my pillow and look at her.

"Does it make a difference?" I ask. "She's gone, which is what you wanted."

I think she might hit me but she scrapes her chair backwards, leans into it and crosses her arms, all the while still glaring.

"You're a cold, unfeeling bastard." Her words, when they come, are controlled and her voice is now smooth as silk. "I bet I could tell you something that would give that heart of yours a good kick, though." She rushes on, not waiting for me to reply or even tell her if I'm interested in whatever else she has to say. Although I am, of course I am.

"It was all for nothing anyway, *she* might be gone, but now he's got a new tail to chase."

Mary lets her words hang in the air between us. She looks almost triumphant now, and I know she is waiting for me to put the pieces of her puzzling words together. And I do, surprisingly quickly for the state I am in. But I don't believe her words. For some reason she just wants to hurt me, I don't know why considering I done what she asked of me, and I tell her as much.

"Patsy McCreesh, he's the officer who saw them at it with his very eyes," she barks, voice control gone now as she plucks her handbag off the back of her chair and stands up. "I'm sure some of these wardens know the story, everyone else seems to!"

She stalks away, out of sight, and I hear doors banging all the way down the corridor. I lever myself up to a sitting position and with a lot of effort I swing my legs over the side of the bed.

She can't tell me this and then leave. I need to know the truth, although I'm certain I already know in my heart.

"Screws!" I shout, although not as loudly as I would have liked. "Get me a guard in here. NOW!"

My wife wouldn't do that to me.

However reports must be confirmed.

Bron wouldn't do that to me.

But I must double check.

But I know.

I *know*.

Chapter 29

April 22nd 1981

The funeral of Rose James is to be held at The Church of the Sacred Heart and Saint Catherine. Thank God it's not Saint Mary's, the same one that Billy is buried in, thinks Mary, what a hateful thought it would be to have the girl laid to rest in the same sacred ground as him.

Mary doesn't think they should go. Connor says that since Rose was living with them, and died in their home, they have to go.

She doesn't know what reaction they'll get, but she can pretty much guarantee that Bronwyn will come off worse than anyone. The gathered crowds may look down on Connor, but not with the same distaste. He's a man, a good looking man, sowing his seed is expected. Women are different; their legs should open for their husband and certainly not for the partner of their best friend. She tells Connor this, in case he is anxious about it, but he only stares at her with unconcealed dislike.

"Don't talk about her like that," he says.

Her heart sinks at his reply. Please God don't let him be falling for her, she can't do it all again, she can't face all the work of getting rid of another woman.

The thought is still on her mind when they arrive for Rose's funeral. They didn't arrange it, her and Connor, she presumes it was left to the mother. And her assumptions would seem to be correct, notes Mary as she glances around at the handful of people gathered there. What a sorry state of affairs, to have less than a dozen people send you off. She's seen the processions of the dead Provo's, crowds of hundreds, no, thousands that are five or ten people deep, lining the streets. This, the service for a young woman, is pitiful.

At least there's not likely to be any trouble, she thinks, with relief, as she settles back and watches the mourners.

The mother, Kathleen, is there. She's heard reports of the woman and her vicious temper and foul tongue, but there is no evidence of that today. She looks meek and dazed, standing alone until Bronwyn's mother moves over to stand beside her. Kathleen doesn't acknowledge her, and hats off to Alia for even attempting to show her support. Mary comments on this to Connor, perversely almost enjoying the strange show now that it's clear nobody is looking her at her.

He doesn't answer. His eyes are on Bronwyn, standing on her own a little way behind her mother. She's keeping to herself, eyes downcast, and to Mary she doesn't look like her world has crashed down around her. Even though the woman has made little effort in her appearance she cuts a striking figure. Her thoughts turn unbidden to the pathetic corpse-like man in the prison hospital. What has become of him? Has he gone downhill since she last saw him? Is he shrinking into oblivion while his wife blooms? Her thoughts are interrupted by Connor moving away and she grabs his arm.

"Where are you going?" she asks, in a low voice.

He shakes her hand off and without answering his mother he makes his way over to where Bronwyn stands alone.

She narrows her eyes as she regards them. She's slipped a pair of big, dark shades on, very Jackie O, think Mary with a sneer. Connor's head is tilted as he speaks unheard words, his hand comes out, rests lightly upon the base of Bronwyn's spine. Bronwyn doesn't seem to reply, but Mary inhales sharply as she moves closer to him, her head resting on his shoulder.

Sensing that she is being watched herself, Mary averts her eyes. She meets the gaze of Alia and holds it. How does she feel, Mary wonders, about the whatever-it-is between her daughter and Connor? Could she be an ally to Mary?

Probably not, she would imagine that Bronwyn has her mother wrapped around her little finger. No, there's only one person that can sort this new development out and though she is loath to go there again, Mary knows she will have to revisit Danny.

Chapter 30

April 28th 1981

Bronwyn sits in darkness in the living room. The fire is lit, the proper fire, the plug in three bar heater has been dispatched to the bedroom. It's cosier in here now and she wonders why they ever let their wood collecting ritual slide.

She looks at her watch and sees that it is almost 8 a.m. She has to go out today, for the first time since the funeral. She doesn't want to but there are things to be done that she can't keep putting off. She's not even dressed yet. But last night she bought her clothes downstairs so she could put them on and slip out unnoticed. Retrieving her clothes she spreads them out in front of the fire to warm as she slips out of her dressing gown. As she is pulling her jeans on she pauses as she hears a tell-tale creak from upstairs. With one leg in she waits, and sure enough, moments later, the door to the living room opens.

"Hello," she says, hurriedly pushing her other foot through and pulling them up at the same time as reaching for her shirt.

"What are you doing that for?"

She looks over, her face warm, her resolve to leave the house weakening. "Doing what?"

"Getting dressed," he smiles and walks over to her. "That's a stupid thing to do."

"I have to go out, I won't be long," she protests as he slips her shirt back off and kicks it across the room.

"It can wait." His voice is muffled as he presses his face into her neck and backs her to the sofa, pushing her down onto it.

Half-heartedly she pushes her hands at his chest, but he is stronger than her and she gives in and lies back as his body covers hers.

She fists her hands into his hair and pulls him to her breast as his name falls unbidden from her lips. "Connor, *Connor*..."

He hasn't been back to Mary's house since the funeral, and she can't believe she had dreaded seeing him so much. He had been so kind, he hadn't cared what anyone thought when he came to speak to her at the graveside.

"I'm so sorry this has happened to her," he had said softly into her ear. "But I'll never be sorry for what we done, Bronwyn."

She weakened whenever he said her name. It sent thrills shooting through her and she had put her head on his shoulder as relief flowed through her. They had stayed like that and she had been dimly aware of the odd little group of mourners. Alia standing beside Kathleen, a silent support though Rose's mother hadn't even acknowledged her, hadn't so much as glanced at any of them. And a little way away, Mary, standing stiffly, sour faced as she openly glared at her son and Bronwyn, and Bronwyn swore she could taste the venom that Mary was breathing their way. Eventually they had left and when they reached the gate Alia had turned around.

"I'm going to follow her home," she said, in a stage whisper, gesturing towards Kathleen who had continued walking. "Will you be all right?"

Bronwyn had nodded, yes, with Connor's hand planted firmly on her back, a guiding support and show of solidarity. Yes, if he and his hand were there she would certainly be all right.

Alia trotted off after Kathleen and with an unspoken agreement, Bronwyn and Connor turned left and started off towards Kidds Road.

At the end of Milltown Street Bronwyn glanced over her shoulder. Mary stood at the gates, alone, and Bronwyn flicked her head back to face front, shuddering from the expression in Mary's eyes.

*

With Connor sated and dozing on the sofa, Bronwyn dresses quickly and quietly leaves the house. Standing on the doorstep she looks around the street. The weather has turned a little bit, it is a few degrees warmer than it has been and a few of the street's residents are out in their gardens, plucking weeds and chatting over the fences. She doesn't want to give them the chance to have a go, so putting her head down, she strides purposefully down the road towards the bus that will take her to The Maze.

Chapter 31

April 28th 1981

It's a big day today; the personal secretary to Pope John Paul II is visiting Bobby. Prison life carries on as normal, but outside is a hive of activity as the public await Father Magee's arrival. I have a visitor of my own however, and as she approaches, I watch her warily.

She's looking damn good. I know I look like hell, and it's like all the fervour that I had a few months ago has been sucked out of me and passed to her. I turn my head away as she sits in the chair by my bed. I can smell him on her.

"How are you, Danny?"

So it's true. Mary Dean's words were the truth and I want to hurt Bronwyn so badly. Three months ago I would have smacked her, I would have knocked some sense into her. Now I'm so weak I couldn't even slap my own face. I could cry right now, but I can't waste precious fluid that I've tried so hard to get inside me in the first place, so I stay quiet.

"I need to talk to you," she carries on, regardless of my silence. "I need to tell you something."

"I already know," I say. I hadn't meant to speak so soon. "I know it all, Bronwyn."

She cries a little at that and I watch her as she drags her sleeve across her eyes. Since Mary told me I've been holding my fury in, but now that my wife is here, I can't seem to dredge it up.

"It was the shock, of Rose," she pauses and looks at me through red rimmed eyes. "You know she killed herself?"

"Shock, fucking shock!" I hiss the words at her. "The fucking pig saw you at it before he even knocked on the door with the news."

She hangs her head and I laugh then. She looks at me with unease. And as much as I know I shouldn't say anything, my remark tumbles out of my mouth. "She didn't kill herself, it was a *hit*. Come on, Bronwyn, Rose wouldn't have the guts to do something like that. And you," I spit as I jab my finger towards her. "You'll be next if you carry on with that prod bastard."

She stares at me, the tears drying on her face, her mouth a questioning circle. She's trying to work out whether I'm serious or not. I clamp my lips together to prevent me saying anything else. She shifts, tosses her hair over her shoulder.

"They've been speaking to me about medically intervening," she says. "And I won't, you know. I'll let you go."

I raise my eyebrows at her and realise I'm almost enjoying our little exchange. This is what we are, sparring partners, roiling rows that ended up in sex. This is what we *were*.

"Good," I say. "That's all I wanted to hear and you should applaud yourself, you're the only next of kin who is willing to let their man die. Good for you."

My words come out petty and spiteful, childish even, but I do mean them.

"Who put out a hit on Rose?" she asks, suddenly, as though my earlier statement has only just impacted her. "Were you pissing around when you said that? I know it wasn't you, Dan, you had nothing against *her*, you shot Connor, you wouldn't go after her."

There's an itch at the top of my spine and I lift my right hand but it's too awkward, I'm too weak and I feel like my arm might snap in two. "Get that for me, Bron, will you?" I ask and heave myself over to my left side.

I can feel her staring at my paper thin skin. No doubt she can count every knob of my spinal cord. The silence and inactivity hangs around us like a bad smell. After a while I hear the rustle of her movement, then her weight as she sits on the bed. She hits the spot straight away, raking her nails up and down like I've had her do so many times before. In all those times I've never felt her tears drip onto my skin the way I do now.

I shouldn't have had her do this because I'm no longer dying in a prison hospital, but I'm at home, in my own bed in my own room in my own house. Moaning that it's too cold and Bronwyn is scratching at me, putting her head close to mine, giggling, "I know how to warm you up..."

And we'll never have that again and maybe for the very first time it hits me what I had with Bron, our house, my old job, Alia even. They were constants, no matter what happened, they would always be there and one by one I've ditched them all.

"I will intervene," her voice cutting through the quiet and my melancholy, startling me. "I'll make them feed you, Danny Granger."

I roll over onto my back and she pulls her arm away. I shake my head. "Please, don't. There's no point in all this if you do that."

"There's no point in any of this!" she cries out. The spell is well and truly broken.

Summoning every last bit of strength I have I grab her arm and pull, yanking her over to me.

"There can be other hits, you know, Bronwyn," I hiss. "I've got nothing to lose any more."

She tears her arm free and she's gone. Just like with Mary I can hear the doors slamming shut all the way down the hall.

Chapter 32

April 28th 1981

Mary gave it long enough to see if anything would happen. A week is more than enough time for him to have his fill and come sloping home with his tail between his legs. But seven days have passed and still he is there, with *her*.

She takes the mid-morning bus to The Maze because enough is enough. She gets off the bus and finds herself in a throng of people that she has to battle her way through.

"The Pope is coming!" shrieks a woman in Mary's face.

Mary wrinkles her nose, looks down at the near hysterical woman and shakes her head. You'd think it was the fecking Beatles or Elvis who were expected here today.

And it's not quite the Pope, Mary discovers by listening in on other conversations, but his envoy on the Pope's orders to try and find a resolution to the hunger strike. It is rather impressive, concedes Mary, but probably a waste of time given the stubbornness of the men involved.

When she's led through to the same hospital wing as her previous visit, she's relieved to find Danny Granger is still alive, breathing and conscious. The room is as bare as ever, and she can see people moving around the corridors beyond. Doctors, she assumes, ready to leap in lest one of their charges suddenly goes downhill.

"Mrs Dean," he drawls as she pulls the chair close to his bed, "Fancy seeing you here."

He's on better form than her last visit, though he's not looking like he'll last much longer. Nobody has died yet on the hunger strike, but from listening to the reports on the BBC she knows it won't be much longer and they'll be dropping like flies.

"My son is living with your wife," she snaps, getting straight to the point. "I want this stopped, it's going to put him in danger and he's had enough of that."

His face darkened upon hearing her words and he pinches his lips together. "I know."

"Well, Christ, what are you doing about it?" she asks. "Don't you think they're not laughing at you? Don't you think they're taking you for a fool? He has spent every night in your home, in your bed."

"Shut up," he replies, and though his words are sharp he looks like he's on the verge of going to sleep.

"You get your man in to do what you had him do the last time, okay?"

He regards her for a long time without speaking. His stare is so intense that she looks away first.

"Another hit, that's what you want, yes?"

Mary nods solemnly. "Do whatever you have to do, to *her*, you leave my boy alone and let him come home where he belongs."

"Can you leave now, Mrs Dean?" he asks and she sits up straight, expectantly.

"I'll do anything you need, whatever you want."

He looks at her again. "Don't beg, Mrs Dean, it's not becoming."

"Come on, she deserves it, she's humiliated you, she doesn't care about you."

He holds his hand up. "Enough," he says, so softly that she can barely hear him. "There will be another hit. Now leave me alone."

She stands, bobbing her head, almost curtseying to him as she backs towards the door. Before she leaves the room she looks back to him. He has already fallen asleep, his chest rising and falling very slightly underneath the thin sheet that covers him. She takes a deep breath, blinks back unexpected tears. She knows she won't come here anymore. She knows that she'll never clap eyes on Danny Granger again.

Chapter 33

May 7th 1981

With Emma's stones in one hand, a bottle of wine under her arm and the three bar fire in the other hand, Bronwyn goes into the living room and settles herself down on the sheepskin rug. She's alone again, but although it stabs at her heart she knows she has done the right thing.

Bobby Sands died two days ago, and today she can hear hundreds and thousands of people lining the streets for his funeral.

At least Connor won't come knocking at her door today, his face is well known now and he won't risk a beating or another bullet by trying to get through the crowds.

She shivers and it reminds her that she brought the fire in. She plugs it in, angles it towards her and sits cross legged in front of it. No more wood burning in the open range. Those days are well and truly over now. She pops the cork on the wine and lines Emma's stones up in front of her as she drinks from the bottle. No need for wine glasses anymore either. And as the fire warms her cold flesh she leans back against the sofa, closes her eyes, and lets herself think back nine days ago when she dared to dream that she could be happy again.

*

Nine days ago.

She almost lost her resolve when she walked back in the front door and found him cooking in the kitchen. Had it been Danny, he would have still been asleep on the sofa where she left him when she went out.

"Hey, did you get everything done that you wanted to?" Connor asked as he heard the front door close behind her.

He must have been out too as he was cooking bacon, sausages and she spotted a carton of eggs on the side. A pile of bread was buttered and waiting in the middle of the table. It should have smelled great, but her appetite had vanished along with hope when she left Danny's bedside.

"I need you to leave," she said as she stood in the doorway to the kitchen. "Don't ask me any questions, just go, right now."

She couldn't bring herself to look at his face because if she did she would weaken. *I mustn't let him touch me either*, she thought, *because his touch is just as dangerous as his face.*

But he had touched her, he switched the gas off and was by her side, in her face, grabbing her shoulders, demanding to know why, what had happened, who had she seen?

She batted his hands away, backed off down the hall, still looking at the ceiling, the floor, anything except him. "Just go," she babbled. "I'll contact you, I promise I'll explain it all, but you just need to go, you just need to leave, just for a while."

He didn't have any stuff, he'd walked her home from Rose's funeral and simply stayed. At some point he had taken a pair of jeans and a shirt from Dan's wardrobe, and she had pretended not to notice. He was wearing Danny's clothes now, and pushing him out of the door was like getting rid of Danny all over again.

*

He had been back every day, knocking on the door, the window, coming around the back, hoping to find her down by the railway tracks, no doubt. But she had remained firmly inside, curtains drawn.

He had shouted through the letterbox that she'd promised to explain her actions, but she had never had any intention of doing so. How could she even begin to explain it? That even if they stayed together and were eventually accepted as a couple by those who judged them, that she could never forgive herself for kicking Danny in the teeth as he lie dying, and fucking Rose's man while she was busy committing suicide. And Danny's strange threat of another 'hit' had played on her mind. The thought of it doesn't scare her, she's beyond any fear now, but if he were to send someone around, best that she be on her own. That way, nobody else will get hurt.

Feeling a little sick she puts the bottle of wine on the fireplace and stands up. She risks a peek outside and sees hordes of people making their way down Kidds Road.

I could join them, she thinks. *Everyone is looking for Sands' coffin, nobody will look at me today.* Unplugging the fire and slipping a couple of Emma's stones into her pocket, she pulls her coat on and leaves the house for the first time in over a week.

At the end of Kidds Road she finds herself standing next to Sue, her neighbour from a couple of doors down. Sue greets her cordially enough and rolling a cigarette she offers it to Bronwyn. Bronwyn accepts it gratefully.

"What's going on with your Dan, then?" asks Sue, as she lights Bronwyn's cigarette. "I 'spect you don't much care, given what happened and all."

Supergrass. That's what Sue means, but her words are not cruel, she is genuinely interested.

Bronwyn shrugs. "He's still inside, he's on the hunger strike, you know," as she speaks the words she feels a strange sense of pride. Danny's actions are stupid as far as she's concerned, but he's striving for something, which is more than most people in Newry are doing, including herself.

"I know," Sue says as she nods sagely. "My Joe works there, doesn't he? You know, our Michelle's eldest boy."

Bronwyn didn't know it, but why would she? Apart from a 'good morning' or a polite nod, she and Sue rarely speak. And what a shame that is, thinks Bronwyn now, we could have shared a cuppa and a fag anytime.

"He wonders if that'll be his mother coming to visit him? Who's getting the power of attorney then, you or her? And what are you going to do?" Sue's eyes gleam with gossip as Bronwyn gapes, open mouthed at her.

"He hasn't got a mother," she replies, eventually. "He was in foster care since he was a boy."

"Oh." Sue looks sidelong at her. "Who is she, then, the one who keeps coming to visit him?"

Could it be Alia? Her mother has treated Danny like one of her own for as long as they've both known him, but surely she would have said if she was visiting him. "What's she look like, this woman?"

"Tall, redhead, fiery thing our Joe says," replies Sue. "My Joe thinks she was that Dean woman, but I told him not to be so stupid, it was her son that Danny got put away for, wasn't it?"

Sue continues talking, coming to her own conclusions, not noticing that Bronwyn has frozen, roll-up cigarette hanging off her lip. Why would Mary be visiting Dan? She never knew him and Sue is right, it would be stupid of her to go to him seeing as Danny did indeed shoot Connor. All the times that Mary pressed Bronwyn to go and visit him comes to mind, she had thought it odd at the time, something that Bronwyn could never make sense of.

"Sue, I've got to go," she says, snapping back to the present. "Thank you for the chat, and the fag."

And she blends away through the crowd, not heading towards home, but to the bus stop.

Chapter 34

May 7th 1981

My heels have cracked from the constant rubbing on the sheets. I still walk when I can, but I'm stooped over like an old man. It's getting harder and harder to drink the amount of water that I'm supposed to and very quickly things are going downhill. Bobby has gone, slipped away two days ago. He was the first to commence the strike so it makes sense that he was the first to go, but it was a massive blow. I quivered when I heard the news, lay shaking in my bed as my body seemed to go into some sort of shock. And underneath the pain is the disbelief that the Brits actually let him die. If they let him die, it doesn't bode well for the rest of us.

Seany looks at it differently, that now he's gone there will be mass rioting and our people won't allow this to happen to the rest of us. I don't know if I believe him but I respect his attitude.

It's time for me to get up and walk around my bed, but I can feel myself drifting off. I fall asleep to my favourite sound: Bronwyn's voice.

I can feel the sheet moving up and down my arm, it's irritating me, disrupting my slumber, and I open my eyes, flicking my arm to shake it off.

"Danny, you're awake," her voice is filled with... relief? I can hope, can't I?

Then the cogs turn, rusty as hell in my mind. She's here, actually here talking to me, and it is her stroking my arm, not the sheet, moving of its own accord, as I'd thought.

"Oh, hello," I say, delighted that in amongst all the doom and gloom and shitty smells my wife has come to me again.

"Are you all right to talk?"

I nod, though I'd rather just listen, talking is hard.

"Has Mary Dean been coming to visit you?" she asks, and she doesn't seem angry, in fact, I've never heard her speak so gently.

Mary, when did she visit me? Yesterday, or was it last week, or even last month? No, wait, its Bobby's funeral today and he was still alive when Mary last came to see me. And what had Mary wanted? Oh yes, for Bronwyn to be out of her son's life, that's right. I'd almost forgotten about my wife's indiscretion, but did I call Kieran? Like a spinning wheel the machinery in my head turns and with each click I recall a little more information. I don't want to tell Bronwyn what I arranged for Rose, but it is important that Bronwyn also knows how a wife should behave, even if her husband is not there and other opportunities present themselves. I wiggle my fingers and she recognises my signal and clasps my hand.

"Stop what you're doing with him," I say and squeeze her fingers as hard as I can. I must still have some strength as she flinches and tries to pull away. I hold my grip firm, I'm not letting her run away again this time. "He's put his filthy hands on you, and you let him. You're my *wife*." I finish, my voice husky and raw, which seems to have more of an effect than if I'd yelled at her.

"I'm not seeing him," she whispers.

"Bad things happen when your actions are bad," I cough. "Look at Rose, look what they done to her. Stay away, Bron, do you understand?"

Her face is devoid of all colour and she sways a little in her chair. Or maybe I'm the one who is swaying, I'm not sure, but I know I can't stay awake much longer and I need to know that I've made the consequences clear.

A forceful wind picks up, wrenching her away from me and spins her back off the chair, towards the door. I call out, weakly, I'm not done yet, I haven't finished, but it's too late, the door is banging closed and she's gone.

Chapter 35

May 7th 1981

Connor has been home for over a week and Mary has kept a close eye on him. He goes to work every day; she knows this because she's been calling the office where he is still working in an administrative capacity until his leg heals completely. On the occasions that he has answered the telephone she has hung up straight away. If someone else picks up, she asks for him, and makes up a nonsensical question about dinner or what time he will be home.

He has been getting home later than usual and she is certain he has been going round her house. But when he gets back he is miserable, shutting himself away in his room, so she is sure that nothing is happening. Mary wonders about the sudden change of Bronwyn's heart. Was she threatened? Did Danny send his man around to have a word? Whatever, he is home and that's enough, for now anyway.

But how much longer is she going to have to live on tenterhooks like this? And it's not just Connor; it's this house.

As if to acknowledge her thought, something creaks upstairs and Mary shudders. When the girl let the noose take her full weight something must have pulled in the roof beams. Now, all she hears, day and night, is the creaking as the upper foundations shift upon the fracture, which means she is reminded all the time of what happened up there.

Mary scoops up her John Player cigarettes and lights one up with a shaking hand. She can still smell death on the landing as well, even though she's been scrubbing at it for a month. She doesn't want to move out, but simmering below the fear is a red, hard anger that she may have to sell up.

She's up on the landing, scrubbing again when Connor arrives home. She sits back on her heels, wipes the sweat from her face and looks down the stairs.

"I haven't started dinner yet," she calls. "I'll put it on in a minute."

Silence, the sound of the front door closing and then his face appears at the bottom. "It's all right, I'm not hungry."

He doesn't wait for a reply and she sees his shadow receding as he makes his way into the living room. She turns back to her bucket and scrubbing brush and looks at the thick pile carpet. It's ruined, it's not made to be chaffed at every day with a stiff brush. She throws the brush into the bucket, ignoring the splash on her skirt as it hits the water. She puts her head in her hands, pulls at her hair and then covers her ears. She's sure she can hear the girl laughing at her, which is strange, because not once did she ever hear Rose laugh when she was alive.

Chapter 36

May 7th 1981

After she leaves Danny's block, Bronwyn heads for the waiting area, looking for Sue's nephew, Joe.

He's there, as though waiting for her, and from him Bronwyn gets the same impression as she does of her neighbour Sue; open, friendly and willing to talk.

"I want to know who has been to visit Dan," she says. "Is that possible?"

Joe seems pleased to be asked to help, and he slides the visitor book over. "It's all in there, everyone who comes and goes." He's proud of their apparent ability to keep a simple log and she refrains from sneering, instead, she fixes a smile in place as she turns the pages.

She can see Mary's name, two, three times, but it's someone else she's looking for now. She slams the book closed when she locates the name she's seeking, shakes her head at the irony of his surname, smiles winningly at Joe, and throws him a wave as she leaves.

It doesn't take much to find out the address of the name she now has, and just as the sun is setting she finds herself on Kilmorey Street. Kieran Lynch opens the door and she can tell by his expression that he knows exactly who she is.

"Kieran, can I have a word?"

He glances behind him, into the house, and then down at his bare feet as though to say that he can't come out.

"I can wait," she says without breaking eye contact.

He disappears inside and minutes later he joins her on the step, trainers on and zipping up a tracksuit top. "Let's walk," he says, and without waiting he lopes off down the path.

"What happened with Rose James?" she asks as they walk side by side.

As she glances at him she sees that he looks positively sick and she knows she's hit on the right track. Glancing up and down the street she nods to the kerb. "Let's sit here a while."

He doesn't talk for a long time and she takes the opportunity to study him. He's young, a lot younger than Danny, probably not even in his twenties yet. His brown hair is fashionably long, touching his collar, and his eyes are a piercing blue. It's his eyes that she notices most, they are fear filled and nervous, never settling on one object, instead, flicking left and right as though someone is going to jump out at him at any moment.

"I was to scare her, make her leave, because she shouldn't have been there." He stops suddenly and she sits on her hands and stays still and silent, not wanting to push him so much that he flees back home.

"I understand what you had to do, it's your job," she says kindly, though she feels anything but kind at the moment.

He looks at her then, a look filled with disgust. "I didn't do what they're saying, I put the fucking thing up and showed it to her and... and that was supposed to be enough."

"So, what happened? Because she was hanged, you know."

"Not by me, not by me!" he cries, and his face screws up as he drops his head into his arms.

"If not you, by who?" Sensing she is close she takes her hand out from underneath her and lays it on his arm. "Who did this to her, was it Mary Dean?"

When he raises his head his face is even paler than it was a moment ago but now he is looking at her earnestly. "I've seen stuff before, shootings and beatings and the like, and it's fine, you do what needs to be done. But I can't sleep for knowing what she done. It's fucking haunting me."

"What who done? Tell me, Kieran, it'll help to get it off your chest."

He rubs at his nose and looks sideways at her. "Rose did it herself. She took the noose, she put it round her neck and then she just stepped off the top of the stairs."

Bronwyn sits back and breathes out hard. She imagines it, but it still doesn't ring true. She can't believe that Rose would have had the gumption to end it. And the guilt showers her again; how depressed must she have been and yet nobody helped her, *not even me*, thinks Bronwyn. *My lifelong friend and I was so wrapped up in myself I done nothing.*

"But Dan sent you there, yes, to scare her into moving out?"

He shrugs. "Yeah, but Mrs Dean asked Danny to help her, she wanted Rose gone. Listen, Bronwyn," he says with sudden urgency as he swivels round to face her. "You won't tell Danny that I told you this, will you? I'll get fucking shot myself. I'm no snitch, I'm no grass."

Is it her imagination or does he give her a funny look when he says that? She raises her eyes heavenward as the chant starts up in her head. *Supergrass... supergrass...*

She pats his hand. "Listen to me, Kieran. Get yourself away from all this. None of your people are going to survive this. You'll all be dead, as dead as Rose is either from a fucking strike or a bullet or just a long life lived very disappointingly in prison. Get out while you can."

He won't leave though, what other options are there for him? He'll be in all the way and he probably will die before he reaches thirty. It's a depressing thought, but one she knows all too well is a reality.

"One thing, has he sent anyone after me?" she holds her chin high as she asks, the last thing she wants to do is show any fear, and she is surprised when he answers her truthfully.

"I don't know, there's something... but I don't know what's happening yet."

He is telling the truth, she's sure of it, he's practically a child still, unable to lie with conviction. He won't last long in this kind of life, not spilling all his secrets to her without her even threatening him. "Well don't wait too long, Danny's not going to last much longer." She means it flippantly, just to show this boy that she's not afraid of him, but when Kieran glares at her she can see it was taken seriously and for a moment she hates herself. How can she joke about the impending death of her own husband?

"Maybe you should take your own advice and get away from all this," he snaps and stands up. "Don't you be coming round here again."

She lets him go then but continues to sit for a long time after he's gone.

His words hang in the air. Was it a warning, or a thinly veiled threat?

Chapter 37

May 20th 1981

I find peace in sleep. The last few weeks were a frightening time where I couldn't distinguish between what was real and what was a dream. Sometimes it was a fucking nightmare. Strength comes in waves followed quickly by fatigue. I can't see at all now and the blinds are down all the time because even with my eyes closed the light hurts them. Today there was an ache in my stomach and I was carried to the toilet. It was a bad sign, after so long without a bowel movement, when you eventually need to go it is the body's way of preparing oneself for the next stage. My system is clearing out, just like me.

So I'm at the end of my journey. Many have gone before me, everyone is going and I wonder if our deaths are still having the same effect on the outside world as it did for those brave souls who went before me. I hope so, or what is it all for?

Sometimes my wife comes. We don't talk anymore and in fact, maybe she doesn't come. I said that I struggle to define what is life and what is unconsciousness, didn't I? I choose to believe that she does come and she sits, sometimes stroking my hand but very gently, because my skin hurts to be touched now. It was agony when they carried me to the bathroom yesterday, why they couldn't have just shoved a bed pan under my arse I'll never know. A last act of mean spirited 'fun' for them, maybe. Though that's a little unfair, most of the people who work here in this hospital wing have been surprisingly...tender, is the only way I can describe it. They don't even eat in front of us and I have no doubt that they go home at the end of the day and see us in their own nightmares each night.

But Bronwyn, there's a lot I would like to say to her, but my voice has vanished. My throat works, I can feel my Adam's apple chaffing inside, but nothing comes out. I suppose we said all we needed to, but it would be nice to chat to her again. Batting words back and forth, her never backing down from an argument, me either, and eventually settling it in the only way we knew how, in bed.

Would I have done things differently? Hindsight is a wonderful and cruel thing.

Oh, she's off again, I can hear her little sigh and the scrape of the chair as she gets up to go back to the house in Kidds Road to plug in the fire and put melancholy songs on while she pours a bottle of wine down her neck. She thinks I never took any notice of her, but I know her inside and out. I know her better than she thinks.

I try to smile at her, I peel my lips back and they stick against my dry gums. Then I hear her speak but it's not to me, it must be to one of the medical staff. They are always there, I can't see them, but I hear them and by their touch I can feel their kindness.

"Do it," I hear her say, and then, though I don't hear her leave, I know that she's gone.

Before I slip back into welcome sleep I have a funny thought, a memory surfaces. Her final words are the same ones that I spoke to Kieran when he came to see me the other day.

Do it.

Chapter 38

June 15th 1981

It has been a strange summer so far. Nothing has happened; Connor has remained at home and seems to have given up going to Bronwyn's house. The broken beam in the loft still creaks. Danny Granger remains in prison, alive or dead Mary does not know. She no longer watches the news on the television and when she leaves the house, which is infrequently these days, she purposefully avoids the headlines or places where she could hear snippets of information.

And even though everything seems back to normal, or as close to it as possible, Mary can't move on. It's what is not seen that is her problem. It's the laugh of Rose that occurs whenever she moves across the landing, a tinkling, girlish melody, sometimes collaborating in time with the creaking beam to create a haunting musical score. Mary doesn't believe in spirits of the dead but she does firmly buy into ghosts of the mind and the memory.

Sometimes she opens the loft hatch and sits halfway up the stairs. The air swoops in, cooler than it is outside, and she stares up into the dark recess of the roof.

"I hate you," she finds herself whispering.

And she doesn't know who she is talking to, Danny, Rose, Connor, God, herself?

Today she has spent hours in the kitchen. It's the only room that she can breathe in at the moment. The living room, the window which although is replaced is cleaner and brighter than the others, is a constant reminder of the night the rocks smashed a hole in the pane, allowing the cold night and the hatred to seep indoors. And the bare spots on the carpet and the table where bleach eroded them is a painful reminder of the spring and summer where it seems to Mary now, thinking back, that she became quite unhinged through the stress. Upstairs is out of bounds, memories of her in her bed, clutching the quilt tight, straining to hear evidence of stealthy footsteps sneaking into forbidden rooms.

The staircase is her own self-flagellation; it is where she goes for penance. Though she tells herself that she had no part in the girl's death, she knows she has to pay in some way.

It is late now, an ink black sky outside and Connor is having his first night out with someone. She doesn't know who, if it's a girl or his male pals. The dynamic of their relationship has changed and she gets the impression that her son now sees her as domineering and over protective. She's not, she's only ever wanted to be allowed to love him the way she never had the chance to love his father. She just wanted to keep him safe, especially from the girls, because women can be wicked in their ways.

Carrying the heavy glass ashtray, she drags on her cigarette as she moves through the darkness to the stairs. The hatch is open but it is silent for once, and she stills as she looks up into the eaves. Did she not close the loft door earlier? Was it even today that she had it open or was it yesterday that she sat on the stairs, whispering hate filled words and berating herself?

With her cigarette clamped between her lips she climbs to the landing, intending to close the hatch. She can't sleep with it open, at night time the demons need to be encased, enclosed, imprisoned.

The net curtain moves downstairs and hooks over the umbrella stand. Mary pauses on the top stair as the movement catches her eye. The door is open, the thought forms but is not fully processed before figures melt out of the shadows of the bedroom doorways, three, four, five of them, like ants moving towards a dropped boiled sweet on a pavement.

I won't scream, thinks Mary as they gather round her. *I won't give them the satisfaction.*

And she clamps her lips together, determined not to even whimper as they grip her arms and pull her onto the landing. She stumbles, one of them tears the cigarette out of her mouth and puts it between his own lips, grins around it at her. And it's only when she is falling backwards that she looks up. Out of the darkness up there a rope snakes its way over the beams, threading out of the hole down towards her. The intention is clear, just like it must have been for the girl as she stood in this very spot.

They are holding her now, cables ties bind her hands behind her and the rough, frayed edges of the noose slips easily over her head. Her toes curl, desperately gripping the top stair like a swimmer before he performs a dive. As they push her, firmly, squarely in the small of her back, she abandons her promise not to scream.

Swinging through the air her voice is cut. She inhales, building up for another scream and realises too late, there is no air left to breathe in anymore.

Chapter 39

15 July 1981

My life froze in that recovery period of more than a month. It's not even done yet; I'm still taking each day so very slowly. There is a big gap between my almost death and where I am now; my almost life.

I am out of the 'H' Block and in a hospital in Belfast. As soon as I am well enough I will be shipped back to The Maze to resume my prison term. It comforts me that I am not the only one whose family decided to medically intervene in the hunger strikes. I wonder if they got together, all of the mammy's and the wives, or if it took just one person to tip the balance and as soon as that one made the decision the floodgates opened for the others to follow suit.

I can't work out if I am surprised that Bronwyn gave the instruction for them to keep me alive. Kieran told me that she went to see him and though he denies it, I know he would have confessed everything to her. He's so young, too young, really, for all this.

And each day that I lie here I wait with anticipation for her to come and see me. She must know by now the decision that I made, to end the life of the wicked Mrs Dean. Perhaps Bronwyn is scared, frightened that I've become this unstoppable killing machine and that I'm going to come for her, or rather, send someone to her. Bronwyn is so wrong, I would never do that, and all I need right now is for her to come and see me so I can make her see that.

I listened while Kieran told me about the events of the night of the 1st April.

"And she just slipped into it, put her head right into the rope and then walked right off the top stair." Kieran's voice was unsteady, disbelieving.

And Mary had come again, this time with another woman for me to dispose of, but this time it was my wife. She had counted on me to be so outraged at Bronwyn's unfaithfulness that I would do her bidding, but the longer I thought about it, the more memories surfaced that gave me pause for thought. When I could think clearly, which wasn't a lot of the time, I had set my mind to work. Finally I had summoned Kieran again, and given him the instruction.

"Do it," I had said.

And it had been done. It would never be traced back to me, it was simply a sad case of recent events being too much for her, and Mary had decided to follow Rose's way out.

They feed me small solids now, mashed up potato, no different to baby food, they think that they are strengthening me but they've got it so wrong. The hope that she will walk on to my ward is my nourishment. The belief that she will wait for me, wait with me, and stay with me, is my salvation.

Chapter 40

July 28th 1981

He hadn't been around for a long time and she thought he'd finally given up. Tonight he's back, hammering at the front door, moving around the house and calling through all of the windows. She wonders if he's drunk, or if he's lost his mind. She resolves to stay in the darkness and ignore him, like she did when he came around each night after she shoved him out of the door that time.

The flap of the letterbox goes and his voice is clear now as he bellows down the hallway. His words tumble over each other and she just picks out one single sentence; "I need you, Bronwyn."

She wonders if he's still staying at home. A cold shiver spikes at her spine and she wraps her arms around herself as she stands just inside the empty pantry and listens to him. She wouldn't have stayed there if she were him, the place that his lover and mother hanged themselves. That house must stink of death and misery.

The letterbox flap clangs back into place. There's a thud and then silence. In spite of all her promises to herself she comes out of the pantry and opens the front door.

He's sitting on the step, head in hands, and she crouches down behind him, lays a hand on his shoulder.

His hand comes up blindly, reaching for hers and with her free hand she tugs at his arm. He gets up, stumbles inside, and she closes the front door behind them.

By the light of the lamps in the living room she studies his damp face. His eyelashes are spiky with tears. It is impossible not to feel for him.

She doesn't offer him a drink or platitudes, or verbal sympathy, but she kneels down on the rug and before she's even fully opened her arms he is there, clutching onto her like a drowning man.

She feels his face hot against her cheek and as he pulls at her clothing he is silent. He's lost weight, she notices. She wonders if he can see the difference in her body. It's not the runner's figure that she gained back but it's plumper, fleshier. Healthy. He doesn't comment on her, he doesn't say anything as he grips her hips hard enough to leave bruises and slams into her. She lets him, she takes it; she needs it too.

Later, still on the rug, he seems to come to and he looks around the dimly lit room at the boxes.

"Are you leaving?" his tone is high, almost accusing.

"Yeah," she replies, turning over to reach for the ashtray and the rolling tobacco.

"When?"

"Tomorrow." She looks at the clock and sees it is past midnight. "Today."

"Where?"

She doesn't want to tell him, she had never planned to tell him.

He's sitting up now, scrutinising her and she hunches over, no longer wanting his gaze on her naked body. "Are you..?" he tails off, shakes his head and smiles. "I want to come with you."

Unexpected tenderness fills her. This man, he's just lost. All of his life he has had someone looking out for him, looking after him and now there is nobody. She thinks deeply, imagining a life with him. One where they can be together without being judged. But she would still judge herself, and him, and how their relationship began and how they behaved. Wouldn't she? Or would it fade, over time, like memories do?

"I still have so much to do tonight," she begins. "Come here tomorrow, it doesn't have to be early, maybe lunchtime."

He wants to know everything now, has she arranged a place to live, a job? Are they staying in Ireland or moving further afield?

"England, the south," she says. "Near the coast."

"I'll stay tonight," Connor announces. "I'll help finish packing."

She shakes her head. "I've got too much to do," she repeats. "And people I must say goodbye to. People who wouldn't appreciate you being there when I see them," she adds meaningfully.

She has revived him, restored him, and it's quite a powerful feeling as she pushes his discarded clothes at him. He covers her face in kisses and she wraps her arms around him at the door.

"Thank you, Connor," she whispers, before giving him a gentle push.

"Tomorrow!" he calls, joyfully, so different to the man who was on her doorstep just a couple of hours before, "midday."

She nods, smiling. "See you tomorrow."

Chapter 41

July 29th 1981

It's strange to be on this train. Despite watching it almost daily from the bottom of her garden, Bronwyn has never been a passenger on it before. It is almost empty today. Everyone is staying indoors, watching the event of the century as Prince Charles marries Lady Di. It's a shame to miss it, she thinks, though, looking at her watch, this train is due to arrive in Dublin at 11:20, just about the time that the wedding is due to start. Maybe there will be a television in the waiting room. There is about a half hour layover before the connecting train is due. If she were at home today she would be watching the wedding with Alia, at either one of their houses. But she's not at home, yet it feels very appropriate that she is starting anew on the very day when the whole world is filled with such happiness and hope for the future.

There's a buffet service on board, and Bronwyn clutches the edge of the table in front of her. Though they may sell those miniature bottles of wines and spirits, she won't buy those. She'll get a coffee, maybe, or just an orange juice. She needs some goodness, her body is telling her that.

The train slows as it comes up to the crossing at the bridge and she grips the table even harder.

I won't look, she thinks. But she does. She shuffles across the seat and stares hard out of the window at her house. The green curtain is pulled tight across and she wonders if anyone ever sat in this train seat and watched her moving around in her kitchen. Her eyes travel down the garden to her rock. She pats her pockets, Emma's stones are there. They will always be with her, unlike the little pieces of Emma, buried right there by the train track.

"The buffet is open, do you want a drink or something to eat yet?" the voice is at her shoulder but something else has caught her eye in her former garden.

"Bronwyn?"

She flaps her hand, she doesn't want anything. A beat, then she looks round. She is alone again and she turns back to the window.

He is in her garden, standing motionless, arms crossed, looking into the distance across the fields. *If he turns to look at the train he'll see me*, she thinks, and absurdly she considers ducking down in her seat until the train is on the move again. And then he turns, is looking straight at her and she puts her palm flat on the window. His mouth forms her name, his arms drop to his sides, his expression is one of disbelief.

She looks away and then, as the train moves forwards on the tracks she swivels her gaze to meet his once more.

"I'm sorry, Connor," she cries, but he can't hear her.

Alia comes back again, laden down with crisps, chocolate bars and juggling two hot drinks.

"I know you said you didn't want anything, but you have to keep your strength up," she announces as she lays out her wares on the table top.

"Thanks," says Bronwyn, gratefully. And she is grateful not to be doing this on her own.

"Did you tell him where you were going?" asks Alia, and Bronwyn knows she must have seen Connor through the train window.

"No," Bronwyn says, regretfully almost. "I told him England, down south."

Alia, to her credit, doesn't judge her. And she never has, she's just... there.

She turns around for one last look, but the Kidds Road house can no longer be seen. It's behind her now, and she swings back in her seat, looks forward. She thinks about the two men in her life for a moment. One day she may call them, or one of them, but they are so irrevocably entwined in her and as a consequence, each other, that time is going to have to pass before she can see clearly. She hopes that one day they will understand.

"Wales is much nicer than England," comments Alia, still talking about their final destination. "You just wait and see."

Bronwyn nods. "It's a fresh start," she says and rubs her hand over her stomach, feeling the butterflies and the bump that is just now starting to protrude, "Just the three of us."

ACKNOWLEDGEMENTS

For fiction purposes some practices have been slightly altered with regards to the actual events of 1981. Saying this, I did want to encapsulate the essence of Newry, H.M.P Maze / Long Kesh and the surrounding areas during the time of 'the troubles'. I couldn't have done this without the assistance of the following people.

@NornIronGirl1981 AKA Bronagh was a great source of research. She 'tweets' daily using her actual diary from 1981 written as a young teenager living in Northern Ireland at the height of the 'troubles'.

Melanie McFadyean's 2006 article in the Guardian, *The Legacy of the Hunger Strikers*, was particularly informative and helpful, as was Melanie herself.

For many parts of this story I am indebted to Laurence McKeown, former hunger striker and I.R.A member. Laurence kindly answered my plea for help and gave me information on everything from the physical effects on the body of a hunger strike, the reasons behind the protests, correct names and terms and what these men wanted to achieve. He went so far as to very kindly present me with a copy of his own collaborative novel; *Nor Meekly Serve My Time*, as well as a copy of his own Doctoral Thesis. And as the emails and voice recordings went back and forth between us, I was lucky enough to get not only a firsthand account of life during the protests but an impression of everything else that makes up a human living under extraordinary circumstances. From Laurence I got a strong sense of intelligence, knowledge, loyalty and humour. A recent feature on Laurence in The Irish Times (*A former I.R.A gunman and hunger striker tells his story*) by Gerry Moriarty is an absolute must-read.

There are also those who are a constant support over the years;

My parents – Janet and Keith, my partner, Darren and my family and friends both in my personal life and the amazingly supportive world of crime fiction.

Noelle Holton of www.crimebookjunkie.co.uk whose cover reveals of J.M Hewitt novels are done with such gusto and genuine enthusiasm.

The fact that she is such a huge supporter of all things crime related is gratefully acknowledged.

The award winning crime fiction author Ruth Dugdall, Beta reader, mentor and above all, friend, who took an early draft of The Maze on her summer holiday with her – that is dedication.